X X X

Ty looks me right in the face with those dark eyes, smirks at me with those sexy lips, and runs his tongue across them as if he knows how to push every button on my body with a simple look. He unbuttons his pants and puts a hand under my ass. With considerable strength, Ty lifts me up and thrusts into me at the same time.

There's this vicious blending of bodies and strong wills and stubborn characters and for a split second, there's no you and no me, just us. It fades away as quickly as it came and soon we're back to just being human; two grunting, sweating, moaning souls grinding together for whatever reason is important today, filling whatever need has to be filled now. I don't think for awhile, and if Ty tells you that he does, he's lying. He keeps his hand on my wrists, keeps me pinned there while he slides into me with long, hard strokes, tries to bury whatever problems he has in me while I let him fill the empty hole inside of myself.

Books by C.M. Stunich

The Seven Wicked Series
First
Second
Third
Fourth
Fifth
Sixth
Seventh

Houses Novels
The House of Gray and Graves
The House of Hands and Hearts and Hair
The House of Sticks and Bones

Indigo Lewis Novels
Indigo & Iris
Indigo & The Colonel
Indigo & Lynx

The Huntswomen Trilogy
The Feed
The Hunt
The Throne

She Lies Twisted

Hell Inc.

DeadBorn

A Werewolf Christmas (Short Story)

Broken Pasts

Tasting Never

C.M. Stunich

Sarian Royal

Tasting Never

For information address Sarian Royal Indie Publishing, 1863 Pioneer Pkwy. E Ste. 203, Springfield, OR 97477-3907.
www.sarianroyal.com

ISBN-10: 1938623428 (pbk.)
ISBN-13: 978-1-938623-42-4 (pbk.)

to the tortured souls whose blood is the heartbeat of the earth.
may you find your happily Never after.

1

Rick is a perfectly nice guy.

But not for me.

Rick is the kind of guy you can take home to your family, show off, and know that at the end of the day, he'll be there for you. I'm not into guys like Rick. I should be, but I'm not. I think there's something wrong with me. I need a guy like Rick to put me on the straight and narrow, to help me stop doing the things I shouldn't be doing and start doing the things I should.

Right now, my back is to a wall and I'm kissing the neck of

a guy I don't know. My therapist says it's because I have 'daddy' issues. Like that's supposed to mean something to me. How can I have daddy issues when I barely knew the prick? He didn't walk out on me and mom like my therapist thinks. She thinks that because I've never told her the truth. My dad died right in front of my eyes, called out my name seconds before the light went out of his face and left him cold. That's all I remember about him. Other than that, my mind is a blank, a series of shadowy pictures without words. They don't make any fucking sense.

The guy I'm kissing unbuttons his pants. I think about telling him to use a condom, but I just don't feel like it. I'm on the pill anyway. He thrusts into me while I'm watching Rick through a crack in the door. He's drinking punch, not alcohol, and smiling with big, wide teeth in a face that's handsome, but not too handsome. Rick's the kind of guy that your friends compliment you on, tell you he's gorgeous, but they never try to sleep with him. The ones they really want, the dangerous ones, the ones with pasts that burn like fire and melt everything around them … Those are the guys that I always seem to fall for. The one I'm having sex with right now is one of those. I don't even know his name.

"I love you," the guy says over and over, and I roll my eyes. I've heard it before, a hundred times, and I just don't want to hear it anymore. I pretend to have an orgasm, moaning and groaning and scratching his back, and all the while, I'm watching Rick. We have a date tomorrow night that I think I'm going to cancel. I thought maybe I'd take Rick out, see how chivalrous he really was, but tonight, he's wearing khaki pants and a red sweater. I don't date guys like Rick.

The guy I'm fucking finishes and tells me how great I am. Then he disappears and I don't see him again, not that night or any other. I light a cigarette and leave the room before any of the drunken idiots at the party stumble in and find me there with my panties around my ankles. I step out of them and stuff them in my pocket, aware that my skirt is too short and that my ass is hanging out. I just can't seem to find it in myself to care.

"Hey," Rick says, intercepting me before I can reach the front door. "We still on for tomorrow night?" He looks me up and down, and I can see that he's curious about my disheveled appearance, my mussy hair and my swollen lips, but he doesn't ask about it. I don't think he even gives it a second thought. Rick doesn't know that girls like me exist. He's heard about them on TV, maybe even masturbates to them, but he doesn't really believe that they exist in this world or any other. I really should keep my date with Rick, go out with him, and grow up.

"I can't," I say, biting my lip seductively and touching his cashmere sweater with a shaking hand. I don't know why it's shaking, but I don't like it, so I pull it back and let it fall to my side. I blow cigarette smoke in Rick's face which is rude, but that I do anyway. There's a monster inside of me, eating little bits of me everyday, and I can't seem to stop it. It makes me do things I don't want to do, say things I don't want to say. It makes me tell Rick that I've got to study for a test that he really believes I have.

I kiss him on the lips and leave an orange-red stain before I walk out the door and down the front steps. People wave at me as I go by and say they'll see me around, but I don't really know who any of them are, so I avoid their stares and their friendly smiles. It's all fake, just a big load of shit that I can't buy into or I'll die. If I ever believe in something again, and it turns out to be false, then not only will my body crumble beneath me, but so will my soul. I'll disintegrate, disappear into the wind and blow away. I'll be nothing. I'll blank out and the energy of who I was will just go away, melt into the ground and come back as something unimportant, like a dandelion or a caterpillar. I can't find it in my heart to care.

I walk back to the dorms because I don't have a car. My roommate isn't home which doesn't surprise me. She's in love with another girl, one that's straight as an arrow. They have sleepovers in her dorm room and 'practice' kissing one another like they're in high school or something. That's fine with me because it means I have the room all to myself, gives me a chance to be alone. I feel most comfortable that way. When you're alone, there's nobody there to hurt you or let you down. It feels too good to have that guarantee of solitude.

I fall on my back on the bed and try to breathe through the tears that come to me unbidden. I don't want them, never asked for them. I couldn't even tell you what I was crying over or why. I just do. Every night, I lay here and I try to find something in myself to live for. Every night, I fail and wonder if I need a guy like Rick to show me the way. But then, I'm a big girl, and a feminist, too, so why do I think a guy could save my soul?

I never thought to wonder if I was looking at it the wrong way, if maybe it wasn't a guy that I was looking for, just a person. And maybe I didn't need them to save my soul, just to give me the other half of it. Maybe that was it?

2

The next morning I wake up and have to force myself out of bed. It's a weekend which makes things so much worse. On days when I have class, I have a purpose, an obligation that I have to fulfill. On weekends, I just wait around for something to happen. Today, my roommate comes home early looking happier than usual. I wonder if she scored with the other chick, but I hope not. If so, then she's setting herself up for failure because that girl, whose name I don't know, is the type that grows up and looks for a guy like Rick. They get married and have babies and think they're happy because that's what people like Rick and this other girl do. They think they're happy because they don't know any better. I do. Not because I know what it's like to be happy, but because I know what it's like to be miserable. If you live your whole life in the darkness, then you don't have any trouble recognizing the light.

"There's a party at one of the frat houses tonight, do you want to go?"

"Which one?" I ask. Lacey, my roommate, doesn't know because she doesn't give a shit about frat houses. She doesn't give a shit about men at all. I wish I was like her. Maybe if I was into girls, I'd have an easier time falling in love with someone that wasn't a complete piece of shit? But then again, Rick isn't a complete piece of shit, and I don't want to fall in love with him either.

Lacey shrugs and takes off her sweater, tossing it over her computer chair.

"It's tonight at six, do you want to go?"

"Any party that starts at six is a party that I'm not interested in," I tell her as I stand up and stretch. Lacey gives me a weird look, and I notice that my skirt's ridden up a bit. I push it down and gather up some clothes. I feel disgusting. I didn't change last night, and I can feel that guy's sweat all over me.

"Come with me, please," Lacey begs, and I know she's afraid to go alone because her girlfriend might ignore her and run off with some frat boy. It's happened before. "I'll give you twenty bucks."

"Keep your money," I tell her as I grab a towel and the basket that holds my shampoo. "I'll go, okay? I'll meet you here tonight."

"Five thirty," Lacey says to me with a smile as she brushes a comb through her pretty, blonde hair. "I don't want to be late." I try not to roll my eyes and tell her that nobody gives a fuck if you're late to a frat party.

"Sure," I say as I leave the room in a hurry, rushing to get to the bathroom before everyone else does. There's this communal atmosphere that descends over the room when there's more than three girls in the bathroom at one time. I don't understand it, and it makes me uncomfortable. I never join in the conversation and have to use the stall at the very end, the one with the broken faucet, so I don't have to look at them looking at me and wondering what the hell is wrong.

I get to the bathroom just in time and manage to shower, get dressed, and put on makeup before anybody else comes in. When they do, they're all wearing blue and yellow face paint and talking about *the game.* I don't know if it's football or basketball or baseball, but what I do know is that it's an integral part of their lives that I don't understand. I leave as quickly as I can and head back to my room, toss my stuff on the floor next to my bed, and stand there for a very, very long time.

When I spy the book on the desk next to my bed, I feel a sense of relief. Reading. I can get lost in a world and spend days there. Besides, reading a book gives me a goal. It's that sense of purpose that puts a temporary bandage over my uncertainty and lets me waste away the rest of the day without anymore negative thoughts.

3

I put on a red dress for the party, something that matches my hair and brings out the green flecks in my hazel eyes. I don't wear tights or underwear, just a nice set of heels and a coat that has a hidden pocket on the inside, somewhere I can put my wallet.

Lacey drives us which is nice because it's too cold outside to walk. When we get to the party, I see Rick standing out on the front lawn, talking to Lacey's girlfriend. It's too much for either of us to handle, so Lacey takes us to a bar instead.

I'm not more than three feet in the door when I spot him.

There's a guy standing in the back corner. He's wearing a black T-shirt and a pair of low cut jeans that emphasize the curve of his ass. His arms are covered in tattoos and his hair is black and spiky, gelled up enough that I know he cares but not enough that I think he wasted time slaving over it. This is the kind of guy I like. I know that before he turns around and sees me staring at him. His dark eyes and suggestive smirk tell me that this is the kind of guy that cheats on you when your back is turned and that spouts a lie with every other word he says.

Unfortunately, this is the kind of guy that I want. At least temporarily. I'm never looking for something long-term, usually just a few weeks or even a few hours. Thanks to my red dress, I don't have to think up anything to say. The guy walks right across the room and pauses next to me. Lacey is already gone, hitting on some chicks near the pool tables.

"Hi, I'm Ty," he says and his voice oozes over me and fills all the little cracks in my psyche. If Rick were to do that, if he could ever even think to do that, maybe he could glue me back together, keep me in one piece? This Ty, this person with wicked sexy lips and arms that curve with gentle swells of muscle, fills my cracks with foam that expands and breaks me into a million pieces.

"I'm Never," I say and do my usual explaining thing that people need when they hear my name. "Never is my first name. I don't give out my last name to strangers." Ty smiles and I can't help but feel this surge of heat in my lower belly. The woman in me wants the man in him. She doesn't care why or how or if he'll even be there later. I hate her for that. I hate myself and my hormones, and I hate men. I hate everybody.

Ty reaches out and takes a strand of my hair between his fingers. His nails are rough and cracked like maybe he does hard labor or something.

"Do you want to dance, Never?" he asks me, and I look around him at the empty expanse of floor between us and the bathrooms.

"This is a bar, not a club," I say to him as I reach inside my coat and find a piece of gum. I like to chew gum when I'm around other people. That way, if I run out of things to say then I can always blow a bubble or something, pretend that I'm busy even though I'm not. "You can buy me a drink though."

"Are you sure you're legal?" Ty says, and I don't like his attitude. He didn't like that I turned him down for a dance. I bet that's his best pickup line. Girls probably think it's cute. I bet he scores a lot by using it. I don't need pickup lines to score, so if Ty doesn't want to play then I'll find somebody else. I shouldn't be thinking like that. I don't *need* to fuck somebody, but at least if I do, then there'll be one, tiny, little second where I feel like somebody cares about me, even if it isn't true. Plus, seeing Ty has made me horny and I can feel my thighs clenching in anticipation. They want him almost as much as I do.

"Cute," I say as I shrug my jacket off and let him see my shoulders. I have nice shoulders, smooth and covered with a dusting of pale freckles. Guys go nuts for them. Ty sees them alright, and his eyes travel down to my chest, searing me with heat. "I bet you say that to all the girls."

"Maybe you're right?" he says, as he drops my hair and takes a step back. "Are you jealous?"

"Hardly," I say as I try to move forward. Ty blocks my path.

"Want to go somewhere else, somewhere we can dance?" I

stare at him, wondering if he's really serious. He's cute, but he can't function without his pickup line. That's a bad sign. Still, maybe he'd be interested if I asked him outside.

"We can go somewhere else," I say to him, closing the distance between us and standing on my toes. I let my heels rise off of the dirty floor as I press my lips to the smooth line of Ty's jaw and put a smoldering kiss there. "But I don't want to dance." Ty looks down at me and smiles. When he does this, he gets dimples in his cheeks that make my heart palpate painfully. Something about other tortured souls calls to me, makes me want them. When I look into Ty's eyes, I can see that we're exactly the same. He's as wounded as I am, and we're both bleeding all over one another. It's a recipe for disaster.

"No," Ty says and although I can see in his eyes that he still finds me attractive, a light goes off somewhere in there. He isn't interested anymore. I've failed some kind of weird, little test that he likes to give to girls. "But that's alright. Enjoy your night, okay?" I watch him turn away, dismissing me just like that. It turns on this faucet of rage inside of me, and I just want to throw myself at him, tear at his pretty hair and the earrings in his nose and I want to rip them out and smash them with my heels, grind them into dust beneath my feet.

"Yeah, that's alright," I say, feeling so mean I can't stand it. I don't feel like myself when I'm acting like this, but I can't let him walk away from me like that. This is why I hate people, even when you have the lowest of expectations, they let you down. "Because I don't pay for it anyway." Ty stops walking and turns around.

"Are you calling me a whore?" he asks and then just shakes his head. He holds up his hands which are so covered in rings and bracelets that they jingle. "You know what," he continues as he opens his eyes wide and looks straight at me. "Just forget about it. You're not worth it." Ty turns away again, and I let him go. My heart is pounding so hard against my ribcage that I can barely breathe.

I'm not worth it?

Why am I not worth it?

"Fuck you!" I call out, and then I'm turning away and pushing through the doors of the bar. I wrap my jacket tightly around myself and walk the four or so blocks to the convenience store. By the time I get there, the balls of my feet are on fire, and I have to pause outside and walk back and forth on flat feet for awhile. The guy inside the store is watching me like I'm a crazy person, but that's only because he's never walked four blocks in a pair of heels. If he had, he'd give me a free pair of shoe inserts and tell me to come on in.

When the pain subsides a bit, I slip the shoes back on and go inside. I don't know what I'm there to buy, so I walk around and don't even care that the employee is staring at me like I'm a thief. That's okay. If he wants to think that, I don't care. Tears are streaming down my face, and I can hardly breathe. I can't stop thinking about the words that Ty said.

You're not worth it.

I want to tell myself that I am, I am worth it, but I can't because I don't believe it either. The reason that Ty's words have cut me so deep is because he's right. I'm *not* worth it. I'm not worth anything. I grab a box of donuts and a six pack of beer and head to the counter.

"Gimme a pack of Marlboro Reds," I say as my eyes catch movement outside the glass doors. I dash the tears away with the back of my hand. "You've gotta be fucking kidding me." Ty and his friends, Lacey included, are coming into the store, laughing and smiling and leaning on one another like they're old friends.

"Hey Never," Lacey says as she pretends to be as drunk as the rest of them. "I thought you'd gone home. What are you doing here?" The girl she's leaning on starts to giggle and gets the whole group going. Except for Ty. He's moved into the chip aisle and is purposely keeping his gaze off of me and on the snack food. I hope it's because he feels bad for what he said to me, but I guess that it's really because he doesn't like me and doesn't want to get roped into hanging out by association.

"I'm picking up my three favorite therapists: sugar, alcohol, and nicotine." This is the only time the group stops laughing, not even the clerk smiles at my joke. I don't look at Ty. I slam my ID and debit card down on the counter and hope there's enough left on there to cover the cost. I've blown through all of my financial aid for the semester and half of my Perkins loan. I tell myself I'll make up for it by pirating my chem book off the internet. It's overpriced anyway.

"Come hang with us, Never. We're going dancing," Lacey says as she reluctantly lets the others untangle themselves from her and go stumbling through the convenience store. It only takes one of the guys a few seconds to bump into something and knock a pile of magazines to the floor. At least the clerk isn't staring at me anymore. I'm getting really fucking tired of being stared at.

"Never doesn't like to dance," Ty says from his position next to a display of Doritos. "She told me herself." I watch him out of the corner of my eye, but I don't stare. If I do, I think my gaze will be hot enough to melt him, to burn those colorful tattoos down his skin, bleed them across the white linoleum floor.

"Are you kidding?" Lacey says, poking me in the arm as I

stuff the cigarettes into the pocket of my jacket and give her a look that says, *You talk, you die.* She ignores me or doesn't get it. Either way, she continues to blabber, oblivious to the fact that I'm pointedly headed for the door. "Never's mom was a belly dancer. She's great at it. Never, I mean, not just her mom." I pause for a moment, tucking the donuts under my arm where they'll no doubt get squashed. Doesn't matter anyway; I'm such a sucker for powdered sugar, I could practically eat it out of the bag. Plus, I have cigarettes and booze. The night isn't a total fucking waste.

Ty is staring at me with an expression that says he's *disappointed.* What he thinks gives him the right to look at me that way is beyond me. *You're not worth it.* I shake my head and step out of the way of the glass doors. They're swinging inward and ushering in a rush of cold air and a pair of guys that I don't like the looks of. There's a girl with them, too, but I don't like her anymore than I like them. I ignore them all. There are a lot of shitty people in this world. I know that better than anyone.

"I'm going to take the bus home," I tell Lacey even though I hate the fucking bus. The campus is several miles from where we're at, and I don't want to walk back alone, in the dark, in a pair of high heels. Talk about a disaster waiting to happen.

"No, no," Lacey says, grabbing my arm as I reach for the door. She's pouting her lips and looks really stupid with her red lipstick smeared around her face like a clown. She thinks she looks cute that way. "Come hang out with us," she pleads as she nods her head at Ty and leans in for what's supposed to be a surreptitious whisper, but actually comes out loudly enough that I know he hears her. "He's single and cute, don't you think?"

"You're a lesbian," I say to her, not trying to be judgmental but wanting to prove that she doesn't know shit about guys. "How do you know if he's cute or not?" Lacey rolls her blue eyes to the ceiling like she just can't believe how difficult I'm being. I don't know why she's being so pushy. We're not even friends, just roommates. Never Ross doesn't have any friends. Not anymore. "Look, I just want to go home, okay? Is that hard to understand?" I push past Lacey and reach for the door when a loud noise sounds from behind me. At first I think that one of Lacey and Ty's drunken buddies has knocked over some cans because that's what it sounds like. Then I turn around and see the gun.

It's clutched in the hands of the new girl and it's pointed straight at me.

"Get down on your fucking knees," she tells me and I know better than to argue. Adrenaline pumps through my blood as I squat down and set the six pack on the floor next to the donuts. Lacey is still standing, and her legs are shaking, actually *shaking.* I don't blame her because these people, whoever they are, are serious as a fucking heart attack. The clerk is already dead, slumped over the glass counter like a doll. His eyes are as empty and lifeless as the dead father's are in my single, lonesome memory, and there's blood, a whole lot of blood. It's splattered across the counter and the floor, glistening red as rubies. I look away from the body and over at Lacey. If she doesn't get it together then she'll be joining the clerk on the other side, and I don't think Lacey's ready for that. Something my mother once said pops into my head at random. *That girl was a young soul; she wasn't ready to die.*

"Lacey," I say as quietly and calmly as I'm able. The girl with the gun looks spooked and the guys behind her, they both have guns, too, whether I can see them or not. I can tell by the way their hands hover around the openings in their coats. The sneers on their once handsome faces tell me that they wouldn't mind using them. "Get down." Lacy collapses to her knees with a thud and slumps to the side. She's passed out. I swallow hard and try to catch a glimpse of Ty and his friends. They're hidden in the aisles, obviously down on their knees, too. Ty is the only one I can see and he doesn't look afraid, just pissed off.

At first, I'm thinking this is just a robbery gone wrong, that if we sit still and wait, that they'll go away and leave the rest of us alive. I mean, the girl with the gun looks kind of freaked out, like maybe she didn't mean to shoot the clerk. Her brown eyes are dilated and blood shot; they flicker around the room like bugs in a jar. Her hair is stringy and blonde with dark roots. It's not a good look for her, giving her pale skin an ashen quality that, combined with the sweat on her brow, makes her look like she's sick. *Drug addict?* I wonder as Ty starts to crawl across the floor in the opposite direction from where I'm crouched. I'm guessing that he's trying to get to the door that's marked *Employees Only* which is fine with me because if he gets out, presumably he'll go for help.

"What do I do now?" asks the girl as one of the guys hops over the counter, shoves the clerk's body out of the way and smashes his gun into the register. Her voice sounds young but rough, like her short journey on this earth hasn't been the most pleasant. I can agree to that, but I don't sympathize with her actions. I'm aching, too; I'm broken, too, but I don't take it out on everyone else. I draw inwards with my pain. Maybe that's not healthy either, but it's better than shooting a man who, as far as I know, did nothing wrong except show up to work today.

"Just shut the fuck up," says guy number one behind the register. He has big brown eyes that probably once made girls say things like, *Ohmygod he's cute!,* but that now look misplaced in his sunken, sallow face. He's got a good jaw, strong and square, but even though I can tell he's young, the skin hangs from his bones like a wrinkled T-shirt. This guy, whoever he is, looks both sad and angry with the world. "You've already fucked this up enough, so shut your fucking mouth. Mel, search the others, take whatever they've got."

Guy number two, the only one of the three whose hair doesn't look straw, licks his lips and gives me a once over. I know I look good in my red dress and heels, and that scares me, really scares me. Seriously though, they can't be thinking of raping me or anyone else here? We're in the middle of convenience store. Surely there are cameras? An alarm system? What about passersby?

"Hey there, baby," he says to me with a leer that makes me want to break his face. "What's your name?" I don't respond. I keep my face neutral, bare of even a frown. If I don't give him a reason to keep looking at me, maybe he won't? Guy Two laughs as he pauses in front of one of the aisles and finally pulls the gun from inside his jacket. It's black and wicked looking, a crafting of plastic and metal capable of changing the world. He bends down and disappears from sight for a moment.

"I think I hear sirens," says the girl as her hands start to shake. The gun looks unstable, clutched in inexperienced hands, and it's still pointed directly at me. If Gun Girl goes rogue, I might not walk out of here alive. I swallow and try not to let fear overtake me. It's a useless emotion, more capable of getting me killed than saving me. Nobody pays her any attention, but Lacey does groan in her sleep, causing Gun Girl to switch her aim to my comatose roommate.

Guy Two stands back up with a wallet in one hand and a new gold watch wrapped around his wrist. Presumably he's robbed one of Ty's friends, but I can't see a thing from my position near the front door. Guy Two is looking at me again, and it's scary as hell.

"Come on," he says to me as he stuffs the stolen wallet in the front pocket of his green coat. "I bet you'd like to play, wouldn't you, little bunny?" No reaction from me. It pisses Guy Two off, I can tell. He storms across the room, boots squeaking on the white linoleum floor, and slams the back of his hand into my face. Pain slithers through my jaw, makes every single one of my teeth ache, and knocks me flat on my back.

"Don't," says the girl with the gun, but she doesn't sound very authoritative. Obviously, she isn't the boss of this trio. "Just leave her alone and let's get out of here."

"You said take whatever they've got, am I right?" Guy Two asks as he looks down at me and licks his lips again. He rubs the stubble on his face and smiles.

"We don't have time for that, asshole," says Guy One as he empties the money into a backpack and then starts in after the cigarettes. "There's plenty of good ass in Memphis. Just grab some stuff, and let's get the fuck out of here."

"Let's take her with us," Guy Two says as I sit up and wipe the blood from my lip. My heart is galloping along at a hundred miles an hour, but I don't let it show. I haven't gotten this far in life to fail now. I tell myself everyday that I don't care, but sitting here on the floor of a convenience store, I know that the indifference, the disdain, it's all a front. Wish I could admit that to myself outside of a crisis. Guy Two points his gun at my face. "Stand up."

"You're pathetic," I say, but I follow his instructions, at least for the moment. Standing can only help my situation. It's hard to feel powerful when you're on your knees.

"Take off your coat," he instructs as he waves the gun around like it's a toy and not a deadly weapon. I shrug my jacket down my shoulders and let it fall to the floor. Guy Two gives me a rictus smile and then brushes his fingers down my arm. I smack his hand away and he snarls, thrusting the barrel of the gun into my forehead.

"You must feel pretty fucking powerful," I bait as I catch a glimpse of movement reflected in one of the glass doors to the coolers. The image is blurry, but I think I see someone moving down the back aisle towards Gun Girl. "So in control of your life. Does hurting people make you feel good? Do you get off on it?"

Guy Two stares at me for a long moment, but he doesn't react to my words. Instead, he pulls back and steps away, turning his attention to Lacey who's groaning and rolling around on the floor. Shit.

"Mm, mm, mm," he says as he steps over to her. He keeps the gun locked on my face, but he kicks my roommate over with his boot. "What a hot, little piece of ass. Do you think she'd wake up if I started fucking her?" My hands curl into fists, and the pulse of blood inside my head switches to deafening.

"Mel," Guy One snaps as he hops the counter again and attacks a cooler full of beer. "We don't have all goddamn day. Get their wallets and let's go." Guy Two sneers and reaches down for the brown belt around his waist. Obviously, he doesn't give a shit about what Guy One says.

"Come on, *Mel,*" I tease, hoping to draw his attention away from Lacey and back to me. "The master calls." Guy Two ignores me, proving that he's the worst kind of monster there is: an apathetic one. There's a moment there where I wonder what the hell happened to make him that way. His hair is still shiny and well kempt, like he hasn't been at this as long as his friends have. His clothes are newer, nicer than even my own. On the outside, he looks like any of the thousand frat boys that I go to school with. On the inside, he's been damaged beyond repair.

"It'll only take me a minute," he says as he lets his belt hang open and starts to unbutton his pants. Poor Lacey is just waking up, just realizing that she's still in hell.

"Don't hurt me," she whimpers as her eyes take in the man towering above her, staring down at her like she's something to be crushed, to be dominated. Lacey, who doesn't like men, who's blonde and petite and dressed in a yellow sweater and a white skirt, who's not the kind of girl that gets into trouble. "I'll give whatever you want, just please … don't."

"They're coming for us," shouts the girl with the gun. She's shaking worse than Lacey now and she can't keep her eyes still. Her massive pupils are moving too fast for me to keep track. "I don't want to go to jail. Let's just get out of here."

Nobody is paying attention to me at the moment, at least not overtly. I step out of my heels, careful to keep my movements slow and innocent because I think if the girl sees me move, she's going to pull the trigger whether I'm a threat or not. I watch the tenseness of her shoulders beneath her leather jacket and the twitches in her face. *Careful, Never,* I think as I switch my attention to Guy Two. *Wait till he drops to his knees.* If I'm going to do this, I'm going to have to be quick.

I look up, trying to catch that bit of movement in the cooler doors again. If Ty or one his friends is back there, maybe they can help me. If they can get Gun Girl, I can get Guy Two, and maybe, just maybe we'll all get out of here alive and intact.

"Roll over," Guy Two commands Lacey as he switches his gaze to my eyes and smiles, slow and wicked, blooming across his face like a disease. Lacey obeys with a sob, turning over and letting herself pool into a shaking mess of nerves and self-pity. He bends down, nice and slow, deliberate, and points his gun at the back of her head. When he reaches out to touch her with his other hand, something inside of me just friggin' snaps.

I launch myself forward without a sound, wound up with adrenaline and anger and fear and I hit Guy Two right in the chest, knocking him to his back on the floor. The gun goes off and fires a single shot towards the front of the store, missing my face by a fraction of an inch. The massive window comes down in a sheet of shards and seconds later, an alarm rings out, sharp and piercing. My ears are already ringing and this new sound is enough to paralyze me for just a moment, just long enough that Guy Two can pull his arm back and use the butt of his gun to hit me in the face. I fall back with a shout, hit the ground with my shoulder and roll away, terrified that at any moment, one of the other two thugs is going to shoot me in the back.

"Goddamn bitch," Guy Two says as he struggles to his feet, and I look up just in time to see that his gun is pointed straight at my face. Another shot goes off behind me, whizzes past Guy Two and breaks down a second window. When I glance over my shoulder, I see Gun Girl slumped on the floor near Ty's feet. He's got her gun in his hand and has it pointed at Guy Two. Guy One is nowhere to be seen, and I can only guess that he's already fled. I suppose that whole *Honor among thieves* thing doesn't always hold true.

Ty is breathing pretty hard, and there's blood on his chest, whether from Gun Girl or someone else, I don't know, but it scares me. However much I might dislike the guy for what he said to me, he didn't flee the building like I'd thought. Instead, he chose to stay and fight. Anyone that's willing to do something like that is someone that the world can't afford to lose.

I panic when I see Guy Two turn towards him and kick out hard, hitting the man in the shin. He stumbles and fires off another shot. I don't have time to see where it goes because the gun is now swinging towards me. People are screaming and there's movement all around me. I think I see a flash of color as Lacey flees the building, but I'm not sure. All I know in that moment is that I have to survive. I don't know why, and I don't have time to analyze it, all I can do is stand and throw my body at Guy Two. I hit him in the stomach, but he doesn't go down, not this time. We struggle for control of the gun, and I pull out every trick I've ever learned to deal with rowdy college guys. I knee him in the balls and pull at his hair with the hand that isn't wrapped around his wrist, fighting to keep the gun pointed at the ceiling and away from Ty, his friends, and me.

It seems this goes on forever, but I'm guessing it's merely seconds. Just as I think I'm about to lose control, Ty appears from out of nowhere and smashes the butt of Gun Girl's weapon into Guy Two's skull. He falters for just a second, long enough for me to knock his gun to the floor where it skids across the tiles and comes to a stop near a display of sunflower seeds. Guy Two uses the last of his strength to push me back; I stumble into the broken glass and feel my feet slide out from beneath me, sending me to my back in the shards with a hiss of pain.

Ty spins Guy Two around and pulls back his fist, hitting him in the face with knuckles loaded with rings. *I hope it hurts like hell,* I think as I watch Guy Two stumble. Ty doesn't stop. He grabs Guy Two by the shirt and hits him again. And again. And again. Finally, Guy Two drops to the floor like a sack of garbage, and Ty shakes out his hand like it hurts. I stare at the wet spot on his chest, afraid that he's been shot and struggle to sit up. Broken glass cuts into my hands and feet, and I gasp, drawing his attention to me. Other than Gun Girl and Guy Two (who are both passed out), we're the only ones left in the building.

"Are you alright?" he asks as he crunches over the glass towards me. I hold out my hand, hoping that he'll help me up, but instead, he reaches under my knees and puts an arm around my waist. With a grunt, Ty lifts me from the floor and pulls me against his chest. The beat of my heart sounds in my ears as I stare at the bit of blood on his face and wonder what the hell he's doing.

"Thanks," I say because I don't know what else there is to say. Ty smiles and looks around like he isn't sure where to put me. The counter isn't an option, not with the clerk's corpse lying so close to it, and I can tell he isn't going to just stand me up somewhere, not with glass embedded in my feet. *You're not worth it.* I swallow hard as I remember his words. If he really believed that though, why is he bothering to help me? Why not just stand me up and leave it at that?

Ty turns towards the entrance and wades through the glass and out the front doors. Now there really are sirens in the distance and already, I can see the flash of blue and red lights. While he's glancing in that direction, I take a moment to pick at his shirt and check for injuries. When I don't find any, I give a sigh of relief. Whoever this man is, I owe him one, and I'd rather not see him hurt. Just when I think his strength is going to give out, he sets me down on the hood of a car and steps back, putting his hands on his lips.

"Thanks," I say again and he smiles, flashing me dimples.

"No," he says. "Thank you. If you hadn't attacked that guy, I wouldn't have been able to get the girl." I shrug because I don't know what else to do with the praise.

"If you hadn't stuck around, I'd have been dead. You could've left through the back door, you know."

"Never even crossed my mind," he says, and I look at him, trying to decide if he's just full of himself or if he's being honest. I decide that it doesn't matter; either way, he stayed to help and that's what counts. Ty nibbles his lip ring and runs a hand through his hair while I struggle to find something to say back to him. I can't come up with anything and start to pull bits of glass from my skin. When Ty reaches out and takes my hand, I nearly fall off the hood. "Need some help?" he asks, and I stare at him like he's crazy. When his fingers reach down and start to pull shards out, his touch is gentle enough that I don't argue.

What is going on? I wonder, but I don't have an answer for that. No answer at all.

4

I let the EMTs take a look at my cuts, but refuse a trip to the hospital. Instead, I go down to the station, sitting quietly in the back of a cop car with Ty McCabe. They want us to make a statement which is fine with me. I want the fuckers to fry, but I know I'm hoping for too much. More than likely, they'll get twenty years tops, ten with good behavior. I try to make myself feel better by imagining how much it would hurt to get punched by a guy with big biceps and knuckles glittering with a dozen rings.

When we get to the station, I see that Ty's friends are already there, sitting beside Lacey in the waiting area. She and I hug briefly and share a look that tells me how grateful she really is. She doesn't thank me which is fine because I didn't do it for her. I did it for me. I get so tired of seeing injustice and pain where there doesn't have to be any. It just bothers me.

I give my statement while the cops try to placate me, offering a trip to the hospital or a ride home, and practically force me to eat some stale cookies from their break room. They aren't suspicious about anything which is nice because I don't feel like explaining my anger to anyone, especially not about Guy Two. It's just there, boiling hot and angry. Fortunately, this time, the cops do their job of playing the good guys and release us after a few hours.

After we finish performing our civic duties, Lacey catches a ride home with her girlfriend who has the audacity to show up with Rick in the front seat of her car. Lacey's face shows this sort of desperate sorrow that I don't understand at all because I've never been in love with anyone before. She pushes it away as quick as it came and throws herself into the girl's arms with a sob. I don't judge her for any of it. I'm in no place to judge anyone.

I don't much feel like going home, so I sit down on the cement steps and put my head in my hands. I'm tired and sore and pissed off, but I'm grateful to be alive, and I don't know why. I had thought I didn't care. Guess that's easy to say when your life isn't hanging tenuously in the air, ready to snap as easily as a thread. Now that I've actually been threatened with losing it, I kind of want to keep it. I wish it was in better shape.

"Hi," someone says, and I look up to see Ty standing next to me with his hands in his pockets and a smile on his face. He's got dimples again and despite the simple fact that I hate him, my stomach flutters in response. "My name is Ty McCabe." He holds out his hand, and I see butterflies all over the back of it, tattooed in a swarm of color from his fingertips up his arm where they disappear under the sleeve of his black T-shirt. "It's nice to meet you," he says, and I can see that he wants to start over with me. I figure we got off to a rocky start, so I give him another chance. *You're not worth it.* I swallow hard and try to remember that I was the one that called him a whore. All he really did was ask me to go dancing.

"Nice to meet you," I say, reaching up and taking his hand in mine. "My name is Never Ross. Printed just like it sounds right across the top of my birth certificate." The silver bangles on my arm clink against the gold ones on his.

"I like it," Ty says, retracting his hand and fetching a cigarette from the front pocket of his jeans. He hands it to me, and I take it, pleased to see that it's a Marlboro Red, the same kind that I smoke. "Sounds exotic," he tells me as he puts the cigarette between his pretty lips and lights it with a black lighter that he retrieves from a different pocket. His brown eyes are watching me with unmasked curiosity. "You were pretty fucking awesome back there," he tells me as he hands over the lighter. I light my cigarette and unconsciously pocket it. Ty notices but doesn't say anything.

"Right back at you," I say as I notice a sign prohibiting smoking within twenty feet of the entrance. I nod my chin at it and Ty and I move down the steps together. We pause on the sidewalk and stand in silence for several moments, watching one another smoke. The two cherries are the only source of light in this quiet spot, just two, little orange glows in the dark of night. No cars drive by and the only sounds we hear are from inside the police station. But at least I'm not alone. If I have to go home and be alone again, I might just break. "I don't much feel like being by myself," I admit to Ty as I study the hard lines of his face. He's beautiful to look at, but he's also broken, bruised, and betrayed. No wonder I was so attracted to him. He's exactly the kind of guy I always go for. I wonder what he thinks of me. Obviously he was attracted to me, too, or he wouldn't have come across the bar to talk to me. I think about having sex with him and dismiss the idea. If he even wants to, then I'll feel twice as alone when he's gone. I admit this, too, not caring what he thinks of me for saying it. I kind of just want to be honest right now. My past has enough lies in it to drown me three times over. "And I don't want to have sex, I just want to be with someone."

"Same here," Ty says as he crushes his cigarette into the ash try on top of a nearby garbage can. "Want to go to the beach?" I nod and copy his motion, putting out my cigarette before following him down the sidewalk. "I don't have a car, so we'll have to walk. Unless you have one?" he asks. I shake my head and pause to remove my heels. My feet hurt either way, so I might as well not even bother to wear them. The EMTs put bandages on me anyway, so I figure I won't be completely unprotected against the grimy streets.

"Nope," I say as I examine my mangled shoes. The heel on one is broken and the other has a bit of blood on it. I feel sick. "I'm in the mood for walking anyway," I say as I turn back and jog over to the garbage can. I shove the shoes inside, next to an empty bottle of liquor and a half eaten sandwich. Ty doesn't say anything, but he does smile.

"So," he continues as I catch back up to him and fall into

an easy stride. Neither of us seems to be in any hurry to get where we're going. It's all about the journey. “Tell me about yourself. Where do you come from? What do you do? What is it that made you want to fight back like that?” The pavement is cold against my bare toes, but in a good way, a way that makes me feel more awake. I like it. I stare down at them for a moment before answering. The red nail polish still looks good and isn't too chipped, despite my scuffle at the convenience store.

“What made *you* want to fight back?” I counter, unsure of how to answer his questions. Despite what he may think, they're all difficult ones for me, and I don't have any real answers to them. I look up at Ty's face, at the piercings in his nose and lip and eyebrows. The streetlights above them catch on the metal and make them shimmer like diamonds. He looks down at me, and I can see that he doesn't know either.

“I'm sorry for what I said to you,” he tells me, and I feel tears sting my eyes. I don't know why, but suddenly, they're just there. I look away and pretend that the cold is getting to me by tucking my hands under my armpits. “I'm the last person that should be judging anyone else.”

“Second to last,” I say, and dash my tears away before throwing a smile back at him. “And I'm sorry for calling you a whore.” He grimaces and the smile falls from his face for a moment. Ty bites his lip and spins the ring back and forth with his tongue.

“That's okay,” he says, and before I can argue, he explains himself. “Because I am one. Or I was.” I shake my head as we pause at the street corner and wait for the light to change. There are no cars, but we wait anyway.

“I sleep around a lot, too,” I admit, and have no idea why I'm spilling my guts to this guy. Maybe it's because he reminds me so much of myself. I reach into my coat and find the lighter and the box of cigarettes. I light up again and pass one to Ty. He takes it in his fingers but doesn't put it to his mouth.

"No, not like that," he says as I tuck the lighter away, and we start across the street. "I worked as a whore." Ty puts the cigarette between his lips but doesn't take a drag. It hangs limply from his frown, and I can see in his eyes that he's tortured by whatever it is that he's done. He looks as sick as I feel. "And not a very good one," he tells me as we pass by brick apartment buildings that were once historic treasures but now just appear rundown. Very few windows glow with light. "For a couple hundred bucks, I would've given you what you wanted." Ty inhales and holds the smoke in his lungs for a long time before he exhales in a cloud of white. "Or I would've. I don't do that anymore."

I don't say anything to that. I don't know what to say. On one hand, I'm disgusted with him. I think things like, *How could he sell his body like that?* and *Doesn't he have any shame or dignity?,* but then I realize that we're just the same, me and him. I may not have ever taken money for sex, but I abuse it just the same.

"I have six sisters which is just as shitty as it sounds," I say randomly, and Ty finally smiles again. He has a really nice smile. It lights up the dark almost as well as the streetlamps above us. "My mother is, like Lacey said, a belly dancer. She does shows during the farmers' market and teaches classes."

"That's cool," Ty says, but I cut him off.

"No, it's not. She could've made more money working at Mc-fucking-Donalds. I don't know how someone could be that selfish and still pretend they care, you know?" Ty laughs, and it sounds bitter and dry.

"I know what you mean," he says as we pause outside a

24-hour coffee shop. “Want something?” he asks me, and I nod as this strange feeling takes over me. I'm hanging out with a guy with butterfly tattoos who worked as a hooker and blew me off at our first meeting. The same guy who tackled a person with a gun just to save me and has a smile with dimples. I'm making a friend. I smile.

“Coffee, black,” I say and Ty grins.

“Funny,” he says. “That's just the way I like mine.”

5

"I had one serious boyfriend in high school," I tell Ty as we sit on the edge of a cliff and look down at the sea below. My coffee is clutched between my fingers, cold now but still good. Ty finishes his with one last sip and crushes the cup between his hands. "We dated right up until the day I ran away. I still think about him sometimes."

"What was his name?" Ty asks as he sets the cup down in

the grass beside him and wraps his arms around his knees. I watch the horizon and see that it's already tinted with a rosy blush, preparing itself for the sunrise that's only moments away. I can hardly wait. After what happened to the two of us last night, we could use a little light.

"Noah," I say with a smile, thinking of the last time I saw him, waving goodbye to me from the parking lot near the high school. That was just days before junior prom. I wonder if he went with anyone else, or if he was still holding out for me. I guess I'll never know.

"Just Noah?" Ty asks as he leans back and puts his hands in the grass. "No last name? What is he, like Madonna or something?"

"Of course he has a last name," I say as I finish my own coffee and go for another cigarette. I try to hand one to Ty, but he waves it away.

"What was it then?" he asks, feeling awfully bold in this early morning darkness.

"Scott."

"Noah Scott, the long lost love of Never Ross. Why don't you call him? Look him up online?"

"I do way better than that," I say as I copy Ty's pose and lean back. "I stalk him online."

"Ah," Ty says as he reaches over and plucks the cigarette from my mouth. "You're one of those." He puts it in his mouth and smirks at me. Apparently, we're good enough friends now that he can do this. I guess we both did tackle a bunch of armed thugs, so I let it go. I'm a little uncomfortable, but I don't say anything, just pull out another cigarette and light it.

"He goes to school in the same town where we grew up, at the community college. I don't know why; he always had good grades. As far as I knew, he could've gone anywhere he wanted." Ty doesn't say a word, just blows smoke into the cool air. "What about you?" I ask, and he turns his head slowly to look at me. "Any long lost loves?" Ty purses his lips, but I don't think the expression's for me. I'm pretty sure it's for his own thoughts. He doesn't look all that happy about what's going though his head.

"Not a single one," he says, and I can see that he's being honest. In fact, he looks kind of pissed off about it.

"It's not as glamorous as it sounds," I promise, feeling the rush of pain and loneliness that had swept over me as I'd driven out of town and never looked back. Suddenly, it gets hard for me to breathe, and I sit up, leaning over my legs like I'm trying to touch my bare toes. They're like blocks of ice, and they hurt like hell, but I'm not ready to go back to the dorms, not yet.

"It's better to have loved and lost than never to have loved at all, right?" I scoff at Ty's words.

"So says the prick who's never been in love." He stares and me, and I realize how badly that came out. "Not you," I sputter and Ty smiles.

"You meant Alfred Lord Tennyson, right?" he asks as I sit back up, trying to forget about Noah again. Whenever I think about him, I feel sick and start to regret all the decisions I've made. If I start doing that, I might as well curl up and die because I'll never recover.

"Who?"

"I hold it true, whate'er befall; I feel it, when I sorrow most; 'Tis better to have loved and lost;

Than never to have loved at all." I raise my eyebrows.

"You're quoting me poetry?" I ask, and Ty shrugs.

"Why not? Does it bother you or something?"

"I don't know," I say, and we both go silent for awhile. I've had a lot of guys try to quote poetry to me. It always just sounds lazy, like they can't be bothered to come up with words of their own. I don't think that was Ty's intention, but I just don't feel comfortable with it, so I say nothing.

"So do you go to the U?" he asks me, and I nod as I press my cigarette into the ground and toss it into my empty cup.

"Yeah. You?" Ty laughs.

"Me? Hell no. If I stepped on campus, I'd burst into flames."

"It's a Christian school in name only. You'd never know otherwise." He shrugs again and sits up, stretching his arms above his head. I watch his body carefully, feeling that gentle tug in my lower belly that proves I'm still interested. He has perfectly sculpted arms, rounded with muscles but not bulging, and a wide chest that tapers into a thin waist. My body still wants me to fuck him, but my mind's no longer willing to let me. These bad boys that I like so much don't serve my purposes when they're laid out on the table for me to see. Ty's already told me too much. Knowing that someone is wounded and wanting is one thing, but knowing why and seeing it firsthand is another altogether. Ty McCabe is no longer on my radar, not like that anyway. I tell myself this is a good thing because I don't have any fucking friends. It would be nice to have one, especially one that I've been completely honest with. There are no lies floating between us yet. It's kind of refreshing.

"I work at a friggin' grocery store. My life goals lie somewhere between shift leader and assistant manager." I don't know what to say to that, so I lick my lips and listen to the sound of the ocean below us. It's calm today, much calmer than usual, and so peaceful. I close my eyes and absorb the gentle whisper of the waves on the rocks. After awhile, I hear Ty sigh, but I keep my eyes shut and don't say a word. He shifts beside me, and I think I hear him stand. Still, I don't look at him. Footsteps sound beside me, and when I open my eyes, Ty is gone.

I watch the sun come up alone.

6

"Does anyone know what the bloody knife in this poem symbolizes?" the professor asks, voice tinny over the microphone she's got strapped to her face. She walks back and forth across the stage with a small clicker in her hand and smiles like she knows something that we don't. *God, I hate lecture halls.* Even if I was inclined to participate in the discussion (which I'm not), there's no opportunity to do so anyway. There are over two hundred people in this class and no time for personal thoughts. The professor moves to the next screen of her presentation. It's a poll with four options. She reads them aloud.

"Number one: the destruction of the narrator's innocence. It's been speculated that the knife represents a phallic object and that the blood represents either rape or the loss of virginity." I roll my eyes and wish I had someone to send a text to. That's all Lacey's done the entire class. She's sending her girlfriend sappy messages with little hearts and smiley faces. If I had a friend, I'd ask them why a poem can't just be a poem. Maybe there is no alternative meaning to the bloody knife in the poem? Maybe that's all it is, a bloody, fucking knife?

"Number two: there are others in the literary world, myself included, who think that the knife is an extension of the narrator's power, that she's using a phallus shaped object to take back her destiny, to show that she won't allow her femininity to be crushed." I open the polling app on my phone and select number two. It never hurts to agree with your professor, and besides, other than our midterm and final, this is the only way to earn credit in this class; we *have* to vote on these stupid ass polls.

"Number three: the knife can be seen as a symbol of past mistakes. For example, the narrator reflects on her poor experiences as a lover. Some might say that the knife represents her lovers' bodies and the blood, her shame." My professor scoffs at this notion and the percentage of people voting for it drops from eight percent to two. "That's quite a misogynistic take on this piece, but of course, we must consider all the possible viewpoints," she says with a smirk.

I lean my head back and stare up at the track lighting on

the ceiling.

It's been four days since the attack at the convenience store. My cuts are healing, but my curiosity is piqued. I wonder what happened to Ty and wish that I'd given him my number or something. The time we spent hanging out, while short, was helpful. I haven't had sex with anyone in days, and even more impressive, the night after I came home from watching the sunset, I fell asleep without crying. I'm still trying to tell myself that it was because I was so worn out, but I think it's because I found a kindred spirit and talked to him rather than used him.

"Number four: the bloodied knife could be seen as a physical manifestation of the narrator's pain, a show of hurt and the consequences of that hurt. Line six which reads, *And from where I had my start, I had gone, and thus nothing was e'er the same again,* is often referenced in support of this theory. It is said that the knife could've been used to inflict some kind of wound, thus maiming or scarring the narrator." I groan, letting the sound get lost in the murmur of the students around me. They're actually buying this crap, discussing it like it matters at all. I hate my fucking literature class. I'd much rather be in calculus. At least in that class, there's always a right answer. In this one, it's all up to the interpretation of a bunch of goons with degrees attached to their names.

"You sure do spend a fucking arm and a leg to listen to someone talk about penises," a voice says from beside me. I lift my head up and open my eyes to see Ty standing in the aisle with a cup of coffee in either hand and an unlit cigarette hanging from his mouth. "Get up," he tells me. "You took my lighter, and I'm need of a light and someone to drink this with." He hands me a cup of coffee and either doesn't notice the students around me grumbling in irritation or doesn't care.

Professor Alma or Anna or Amy or whatever her name is keeps droning on about the symbolism of the collie dog in the poem and how its black fur represents a vagina.

I grab my backpack and haul ass out of there, pausing for just a moment to vote on the next poll that the professor's pulled up on her screen.

"How do you know so much about my tuition?" I ask as Ty drags me to a small stone wall in the center of the courtyard. It's just about knee high and surrounds a dry garden bed and an old tree. There's gum stuck all over it, but I sit down anyway, folding my tiny, black skirt under my thighs so that my bare skin doesn't touch any of it.

"I looked it up online," he explains as he holds out his hand and passes me a cigarette. "Among other things." I take the lighter out of the side pocket on my bag and light us both up.

"So you're stalking me now?" I ask, but I smile when I say it.

"You stalked Noah Scott," Ty says as he takes a drag on his cigarette and sighs like he's in heaven. They'll make you feel that way, cigarettes will, like you're in paradise while they kill your insides. I wish I could quit, but I can't make myself care enough to go through that much effort. "Over twenty grand just to talk about penises?"

"I have a scholarship," I say as I sip my coffee. *Mmm. Still warm.* "And financial aid."

"How?" Ty asks casually, too casually. He's fishing for information. I take a moment to consider my answer as I sweep my gaze over him. He's still just as dark, as dangerous looking as he was at the club. Even in the harsh winter sunlight, Ty looks perfect. His dark hair is lying flat today, but it's clean and it shimmers like onyx, speckled with flecks of color from the breaks in the leaves above us. His sexy lips are smiling, but his dimples aren't showing, meaning that he's probably putting on a front for me. His piercings are all different today, all silver with white-blue crystals in them. They compliment the gray T-shirt he's wearing over his bootcut blue jeans. They're tucked into big, black work boots with the laces still undone.

I reconfirm my earlier assessment that while Ty is still hot, the ideal male specimen, that I'm not interested, not like that, not anymore. There's still a little quiver in my belly, an aching pulse down below that tells me that my body still wants him, but I don't feel that desperate frenzy to fuck like I do sometimes, that need to fill myself so that I won't be alone, even if it's just for a second. Maybe it's because Ty talks to me, treats me like a person instead of an opportunity?

"I filled out the FAFSA and trolled the Internet for scholarships, anything to do with … " I almost don't say it.

"You can tell me what the hell a *FAFSA* is in a minute. To do with what?"

"Dance," I say and my voice comes out like a whisper, swirls through the air with a cluster of dried leaves. "I had some videos of myself, so I posted them wherever I could." Ty doesn't respond until he finishes his coffee. He wrinkles the cup up in his hand and makes an impressive toss across the bricks of the courtyard. The cup hits the rim of a garbage can and slides inside.

"Show me."

7

I take Ty up to my dorm room which is weird because I've never had a guy in there, not once, not for any reason.

"Cozy," he says, and I can't tell if he's being facetious or if he's telling the truth. I sit down at my desk which is at the end of Lacey's bed instead of at the end of mine. We switched spots because I like to stay up late and type things, not stories or poems though, just things. Lacey says the light of the screen from this angle isn't as bad as it is from the other side. Ty understandably mistakes her bed for mine and sits down on the pink and white comforter. "You know," he says as he pulls open the drawer on the bedside table and peeks inside. Whatever it is that he sees in there causes him to smirk wickedly. "When I asked if you were legal, I was serious. How old are you anyway?"

"Close that," I snap as his hand starts to venture inside. "That's my roommate's stuff." Ty raises his dark brows and stands up, moving over to my rumpled black and red bedspread. Apparently, he thinks it's okay to look so long as the stuff is mine and opens my drawer next. There's not much in there, so I ignore him and search for one of the videos on my laptop. *Why are you showing him this?* I wonder as I search through old folders looking for the last performance I ever had filmed. My final performance, the one I did right before I packed up some clothes and left my costumes and my family behind, wasn't filmed. It was for one man's eyes only. "I'm twenty-one," I respond absently as I find the video I'm looking for.

"Twenty-two," Ty says as he stands up and stretches. "So that means you have, what, a year and a half of school left?"

"Supposedly," I say as I click the video and open it to full screen. I lean back in my chair and watch a girl who was me, but isn't anymore. That girl, the one in the turquoise top and the hip scarf, she's long dead, and there's no way to bring her back. I wonder if my mom or my sisters ever watch this video and think of me? I think of them all the time, video or no.

Ty kneels down next to me and puts one hand on the arm of my chair and the other on my desk. His breath tickles my fingers and make them twitchy. Suddenly, I have this crazy urge to brush the hair from his forehead. *What the fuck is wrong with me?* I look back at the screen and try not to frown. In the recording, I'm doing my mother's homegrown version of tribal belly dance where one lead dancer cues the other girls in the group with subtle motions, telling them what move comes next. It's all improv; nothing is choreographed. It gives the dance a more organic look, like it's something from wilder times where women might've dance around campfires and worshipped goddesses whose names are like whispers on the wind.

I'm wearing a big, black skirt that hangs so low it touches the tops of my henna patterned feet, and a scarf with big, silver tassels that swing wide arcs around me as I spin. My hair is its natural copper color in the video, not black and red like it is now. I dyed it to match my bedspread. At the time, it seemed as good an inspiration as anything. At least my comforter was always there, night after night, holding me, cradling me tight. What else could I ask for?

"You're fucking beautiful," Ty tells me honestly as he watches the video, brown eyes flickering across the screen, tracing my every movement. I don't blame him; I was prettier then, skinny and lithe and muscular with a flashy, blue zircon belly ring in the shape of a butterfly. Watching this video makes me remember why I don't dance anymore. I was perfect that day and even better the next. If I dance now and mess up those memories, I'll never forgive myself. I open my mouth to tell Ty this because for whatever reason, I want to spill my guys out to him, when Lacey walks in the room with a pink shopping bag on one shoulder and a blue one on the other. Her girlfriend is standing right behind her, giggling, but stops as soon as she sees Ty. Then she switches her attentions from Lacey to him.

It's hard to resist a man like Ty McCabe, even for someone as emotionally shallow as what's-her-name.

"Hey there," she says, and Lacey goes from smiley to scowling, twisting her skinny lips into an angry frown. Ty doesn't respond to her right away. First, he reaches over me and wraps his big hand around mine, moving the mouse to the pause button. He clicks it and stands up suddenly.

"Hey there yourself," he says with a naughty smirk that bugs the hell out of me for whatever reason. "The name's Ty," he tells her as he moves aside so that Lacey can throw her bags on her bed. She's on the verge of having a temper tantrum, but nobody notices but me. "Mind if I grab yours?"

"Renee Foster," she tells him with the very same smile she was using on Rick at the frat party only a few days prior. See, I told you girls like Renee want to marry guys like Rick and have kids and pretend to be happy, but they secretly want to fuck guys like Ty. I tap my fingers on my desk and feel irritated. Why, I can't guess, because he doesn't belong to me. I don't want him to belong to me. Maybe I just don't like Renee?

"Nice to meet you, Renee," he says with a dimpled smile and the two of them shake hands. I'm happy to see that he doesn't touch her hair or let her kiss his jaw like he did with me. "You must be Lacey's girlfriend. I've only heard good things." Renee's face turns pasty white and she whirls on Lacey with a glare that could kill. She says nothing, but her breath huffs in and out like a wild animal. Ty and I both seem to know when it's better to stick around and when it's best to leave because we both move towards the door and around Renee at the same time.

"That was totally uncalled for," I hiss at him as soon as it closes behind us. Shouts echo out and down the hallways. Luckily, most people are in class right about now so there isn't a crowd around to hear.

"What was?" Ty asks, going for a cigarette even tough there's a *No Smoking* sign just a few feet down from where we're standing. I stare at his perfect head, silhouetted against the white wall and for some reason, I just want to hit him. I don't know why, I just do.

"Go away," I tell him as I snatch the cigarette from his hand. He looks at me for a long time, just stares at me. "Get out!"

Ty reaches out, takes the cigarette back and disappears down the hallway.

I don't see or hear from him for a week.

8

I'm at a stupid, fucking party with Lacey again because I'm so mad at myself for kicking Ty out of my dorm that I can barely think about anything else. I don't have his number or e-mail or address, and he's been virtually impossible to find. I've searched *Ty McCabe* on just about every social networking site, plugged it into just about every search engine. All I can think is that I've driven my first and only real possibility at a friend away, and now the hunger is back, the gnawing loneliness that brings unbidden tears at night. It's whispering at me, telling me what I should do to ease that ache. If I don't obey it, sooner or later it'll turn into a scream. So I do what I do best and give into it.

I'm hitting on a guy in a black sweater with hair that looks uncannily similar to mine – black with a red streak in the front. He's talking about how much he loves motorcycles and I'm nodding and picking lint off his sweatshirt with a smile. Lacey's standing beside me fuming because Renee won't talk to her anymore. She told me that Renee called her a *damn dyke* and even had the audacity to slap her. I asked Lacey if they'd ever slept together, but she wouldn't give me a straight answer. Doesn't matter anyway, I suppose, because I'm in no place to help anyone else with their love life. I don't even have one of my own.

I slide my hands down the bright blue fabric of my dress, pleased at the way it frames my breasts but disappointed at how much it bunches around my midsection. I'm a lot curvier than I was in that belly dancing video, and it's starting to get to me. I've probably watched it a hundred times since Ty left, and I'll probably watch it a hundred more before I'm done. I feel somehow that it's not over until he sees the end, until he sees my mother make a fool of herself on the stage and set into motion the events that drove me away from my home and into the arms of the real world, emancipation, and a series of shitty jobs that almost killed me. *At least I was never a whore like Ty,* I think bitterly and then suddenly just feel sad for him. That empty, gaping, lonely spot in me is crying out for attention.

"Hey, want to go somewhere?" I ask the guy in the sweater. I think his name is Jason or something, but I don't say it aloud in case I'm wrong.

He raises his eyebrows and says, “Sure thing, beautiful.” I grit my teeth and pretend I don't hear that. I hate that term, *beautiful.* It's so condescending that it makes me sick.

“Hey Never,” says this girl who I know only briefly because we have a lab together. “Your boyfriend's here.”

“My boyfriend?” I ask as I drop Jason-or-whatever's hand and push through the pulsing, vibrating throng towards Shanay. She's pointing towards something, but it's hard to see because there are people everyone, just this big, massive, thrusting, sweating wall of them. Some of them are dancing, others are halfway to a home run, and some are just singing, voices heavy with liquor and pot. I kind of hate it here, but then, I had nothing else to do tonight. I finished all the books on my *to read* list and felt all the emptier because of it. One contemporary romance novel after another slid down my throat until I was convinced that something was wrong with my life. Those girls always get what they want in the end. I'm envious of them. I want an ending like that, too. “Boyfriend?” I ask Shanay. She doesn't really know me, not the true me anyway, but she's aware that I do not date. Not for real.

“The guy with the .... ” she flickers her fingers against her arms, and I know instantly what she means. *The guy with the butterfly tattoos.*

“Ty is here?” I ask, not even bothering to correct her about the boyfriend thing. I'll be lucky if she can even hear me with the rap music drilling a hole in both our brains. She nods and points towards the door. I don't even thank her, just push through the bodies and the youthful euphoria that I'm surrounded by but not a part of.

Ty is standing on the front porch with a beer in one hand and a cigarette in the other. He's wearing a red tank top that shows off his muscular shoulders and highlights the tattoos on his upper back. I see a raven, a bald eagle, a hummingbird. All of them have their wings spread in flight and expressions of complete and utter bliss on their faces. That is, if you can imagine a bird looking blissful. Whoever did Ty's tats was skilled at it.

I touch his shoulder as I step out beside him, and he turns to look at me.

"I'm sorry," he says as he tries to hand the beer to me. His gold bracelets tinkle against the glass as I wave him away. I only drink when I'm at rock bottom. I'm hovering close by, sure, but I'm not there yet. If I drink, I'll only fall faster.

"For what?" I ask as I fold my arms over my chest and try not to shiver in the December cold.

Ty says, "For disrespecting your friend," just like that, and I forgive him with a sigh. I'm bouncing up and down on my toes, trying to stay warm. My dress is made of some cheap polyester blend stuff that I absolutely hate and does nothing to keep me warm. I'm also not wearing any panties; it's not the whole *easy access* bullshit that guys like to think. I just don't like wearing them.

"Hey you." A hand lands on my shoulder and I spin around to find Jason-or-whatever standing there with a beer in either hand.

"Hey you?" Ty asks with raised brows and shakes his head as he sips his Alleycat Amber. I glance at him, but I don't think Jason-or-whatever can hear him over the heartbeat of the music.

"Come dance with me," he says as he practically thrusts the beer between my breasts. I wave it away and try to smile. I did just ask the guy off somewhere and then leave him, but now that Ty's here, I want to hang out a bit. Maybe I'll find

Jason-or-whatever later and we can do it? I just don't know because if Ty asks me to the beach again, then I'll go because I suddenly want to tell him about my sisters. Not just what they look like, but what they do, where they are now, that kind of stuff.

"I don't dance," I say with a shivery shrug. I give the guy a type-lipped smile that tells him I'm done with this conversation and start to turn away. "Thanks but no thanks."

"Come on," he says as he presses the cold bottle of beer between my shoulder blades. "You promised me a *dance*, remember?" I catch Ty looking at me and roll my eyes. He glances over his shoulder at Jason-or-whatever and gives him a *look* that says, *Leave her the fuck alone,* which is kind of cool but that I could've done myself. If I've learned anything in the past few years, it's how to protect myself. I want to know that should I ever say *no* to one of these guys, these bad boys that I pick up at these parties, that I can stop them from taking it further than I want to go.

Suddenly, there's this cold liquid running down my back and I'm spinning around to find that the black sweater dude has just poured foamy beer down my dress. Ty spins around, too, and grabs the dude by his massive bicep. Ty's is bigger which is nice, and he looks awfully intimidating as he tugs the Jason guy towards him.

"You better fucking watch yourself," he says as he gets real close to this guy's face. I open my mouth to tell him that I'll take care of it when he surprises me by saying, "Because this girl is tough shit. She took down an armed gunman, so who the fuck do you think you are? Unless you're packing some serious heat then back the hell off because you're liable to get damaged, do you understand me?" Jason opens his mouth to argue when my hand comes out and socks him right in the face. His nose crumples beneath my knuckles, but it *hurts* and

I hiss as I stumble back and nearly fall off the stoop.

Ty releases Jason-or-whatever and grabs my wrist, saving me in the nick of time from overbalancing on my heels and falling to my back on the pavement.

"Come on," he says as he extracts me from a situation that could go from bad to worse real fast. Without saying goodbye to Lacey, I slip off my heels, tuck them under my arm and take off down the sidewalk with Ty at my side. My arm is tingling all the way up to the elbow, and my hand is throbbing, but I shake it off and pretend that it doesn't hurt

"Thanks," I say, but Ty waves my gratitude away with a jingle of his bracelets.

"Sorry," he tells me, and I can't figure out what he's apologizing for. I also have no idea where we're going, but I follow along anyway because there's nowhere else I'd rather be than with a potential friend. A real friend. My *first*, real friend since I left home. We may not be there yet, but the hope is there; the *possibility* is there. "About stalking you. I figured it was the only way we could hang out since you had no way to contact me."

"Makes sense," I tell him as we continue down the street and turn a corner towards a rougher part of town, one that I wouldn't normally venture into. I'm still sticky with beer and I can make a pretty accurate assumption about the state of my dress. I bet my ass is visible from space through the cheap, wet, fabric. I make myself move faster, practically sprinting through the spots of light from the streetlamps and dragging my feet in the shadows between. Ty reaches down for my hand, and I let him take it, if only for appearances. I brush a strand of hair from my face with my other hand. "Do you maybe have a phone number?" I ask as I step carefully around a used needle that's sticking out of some tired, old bushes at the edge of the sidewalk. It may not have been the smartest idea to walk barefoot in this area, but I don't care. I need to feel the cold pavement against my skin today. It brings everything around me to life and though stark, it's all decrepit beauty to me. "Or an e-mail? I couldn't find you anywhere online." Ty smiles, but there are no dimples. It doesn't even reach his brown eyes.

"You won't. I don't go online much."

"Except to stalk me?" I ask, and his smile gets a little bigger, a little more real. Ty nods and reaches into his pocket. He emerges with his phone and we trade numbers. *Finally,* I think as I tuck my phone between my breasts. Ty doesn't even comment on my hiding place. He's probably seen it before. Any girl with *C'*s or bigger knows she can store stuff there.

"Here," he says as we pause next to an iron gate. There's a security guard at the gatehouse, a computerized pin pad, and everything. I know this place: it's the gated community the city put here in the middle of all this squalor to try and 'revitalize the neighborhood'. It didn't work. All they got was a bunch of pretty apartments in a sea of crackheads and prostitutes that are worth half as much as they cost to build. The city turned them into subsidized housing and washed their hands of it, but the place still looks well kempt, a far cry from its dilapidated neighbors that tower above us on either side like drunken giants. "Come on in," Ty tells me as we move across the pavement and pause next to the guard's window. The man barely looks up, sees that it's Ty and smiles. A nod is exchanged between the two men and the gate swings open.

"Do you have a roommate?" I ask him as we walk slowly across the pavement turned blacktop. The arrows, the parking space markers, the handicapped symbols, are all perfectly outlined and painted in bright, neon colors below our feet. Ty gets out two cigarettes, lights them and hands one to me. If being around Ty is good for my soul then it's bad for lungs. I don't smoke even half this much when I'm alone.

"Nope," he says as he points up at a mustard yellow building with chocolate trim and rust colored accents. It looks better than it sounds, sophisticated, neat, clean, not really the place I expected Ty to be living. In my head I'd cooked up thoughts of abandoned train cars with velvet drapes or maybe a run down bus parked permanently in the RV spaces at the beach. This is all so ... normal, and if I know anything at all about Ty yet, it's that he isn't exactly normal.

"How did you ever find yourself here?" I ask as we continue across the parking lot and veer away from the buildings, towards a small park with a slide, a swing set, and some blue monkey bars. Ty is still holding my hand, but I don't pull away, even though we're now in the relative safety of the gated community. His skin is warm and the smooth metal of his rings is comforting against my palm.

"When I stopped ... " Ty pauses and chews his lip ring. "When I quit *the business*," he says as he slides his brown eyes over to me and I can see he's hoping like hell that I get it. I nod my chin slightly and smile as gently as I can. I'm surprised he's even telling me this, and I don't want him to get spooked and clam up. *When I quit being a whore,* he's saying. "I was living with a client at the time, and she kicked me out. I didn't know what to do, so I started jumping the wall at night and sleeping here." Ty points up at the play structure. It's made of blue and red plastic with round windows that remind me of a submarine. I listen to his words and hope that there's nobody up there now. "Didn't last long though. Apparently, they were between security guards. As soon as they hired a new one, I got busted."

Ty and I walk down the sidewalk that lines the wood chip

filled play area and pause at the edge of a dew covered lawn. The grass is short and well manicured, but there are these tiny, white daisies that have sprouted everywhere in little clumps. With the moonlight highlighting their petals, they look like stars.

"Anyway," he says as he drops my hand and sits down on the edge of the cement. "The guy felt sorry for me, so he set me up in a vacated apartment. All I had to do for my first month's rent was clean it." Ty smiles tightly as he pulls off his boots and sets them to the side. I stay standing, not quite sure what we're doing here but intrigued nonetheless. "Actually, it was pretty fucking disgusting, so I think I got the short end of the stick." Ty laughs which makes me laugh, and stands up, rolling his pant legs to the knee. "Be spontaneous with me?" he asks, and holds out his hand again. I toss my heels to the ground and take it, stepping into the wet grass, careful to keep from crushing the tiny daisies.

"You never finished watching my video," I tell Ty, pulling my phone out and handing it to him. I've loaded it on there in preparation for this moment. I want him to watch it, the whole thing, all the way through my mom's speech until that final, heartbreaking moment when I know for sure that she doesn't love me as much as she loves herself.

Ty takes the phone in his other hand and keeps walking. He wiggles it in the air and flashes me a perfect smile.

"I've been thinking a lot about this, you know," he says, and I smile back. Mine is just as real as his, and I'm surprised at how foreign it feels on my face. I haven't smiled like this in *years*. "I can't get this image of you out of my head," Ty adds as he cues up the video and watches me sweep across the stage with finger cymbals on my henna patterned hands.

"'Cause I'm so 'fucking beautiful'?" I joke, quoting Ty back to himself. He doesn't respond, but his dimples get deeper, just enough that I'm tempted to reach up and poke his cheek with my fingers. He has nice cheekbones for a man, defined but not gaunt. I look away from his face and up at the moon. She's shrouded with gentle clouds, obscuring her shape but not her light. It trickles down and feels cool and comforting against my face. I haven't taken the time to appreciate her beauty in a long while, and I miss it. This all feels good, maybe too good. I'm a bit worried about this new friendship with Ty because if it fails, if he blows me off or disappoints me somehow, I'll shrivel up and die. I've had enough people in my life betray me that I've run out of restarts. This is it. If I give Ty my last chance, then I'll be betting everything on him. I swallow hard and wait for the video to end. Once it does, then I'll have the chance to tell him the truth about what happened at home. That will be his test. If he fails it, I'm done. The cocoon I've built around myself will turn to steel, and I'll block it all out, I swear I will.

My mother is speaking, telling the gathered crowd a secret that she's kept not from my other sisters but just from me. Only me. I was the one left out. The one that didn't deserve to hear her plan. I think it was because, deep down, she knew how wrong it was, but she was – is? – so fucking selfish.

Am I making a rash decision? I wonder as I watch the light from the screen flicker across Ty's face. It's not too late to back out, to change my mind, to save this chance for someone else. The video ends with my mother's announcement about her engagement, and somehow, in some cruel trick of fate, Noah, who is holding the camera, zooms in on my face, catches me at my most vulnerable. Burned into the last frame of that recording is me with my eyes haunted and my mouth open in shock. All around me a crowd cheers and inside, I die just a little.

Ty hands the phone back to me and stops smiling as we circle around the lawn and head back towards the playground.

"What on earth did she do to you?" Ty asks, and my heart pauses for a moment, resets itself to overdrive and starts to pound. This is why I'm always attracted to tortured souls, to people with wounds like mine because once you have them, you can recognize them a mile away. But I've never gotten this close to one. It's terrifying. My hand starts to shake, and I untangle it from Ty's as we hit the pavement. I reach for my shoes but pause when Ty touches a hand to my shoulder. "Come on," he says as he starts towards the swing set. "Tell me about it."

"I … " I follow Ty to the black swings which are soaking wet from the dewy night and watch, almost mesmerized, as he takes off his shirt and wipes the moisture away. When he's finished, he tosses it over his shoulder and holds out a hand to indicate that I should sit. My eyes trace his perfect chest, his chiseled midsection, and all of a sudden, I feel sick. *No,* I tell myself. *I won't sleep with him, not ever, so fuck off.*

"Come," he tells me. "Take a load off."

"I can't," I say as I take a step back. I've only said the thing I want to say twice before and both times, life did not work out well for me. My memories are jumbled and confusing, and I just can't find the heart to put it out there. Not yet. I need more time. "I'm sorry," I say aloud as I take another step back and reach down for my shoes. Ty watches me with sad eyes and nods like he understands completely. I turn away, grab my heels and hold them against my chest. After a few careful breaths to steady myself, I turn back to him and toss a fake smile his way. I can tell that he knows it isn't real and watch as he returns it with a false smile of his own. "Don't be a stranger," I say as I start back off towards the gate.

"There's no way I'm letting you walk out of here alone," he

tells me as he moves around the swing set. "Let me walk you home."

"You're going to stop me?" I challenge, not because I think walking home alone is a good idea but because I don't like being told what to do. Ty holds up his hands like he doesn't know what to say and drops them to his sides.

"I guess not," he replies, but he looks kind of pissed off about it. He sits down on the swing and wraps his hands around the chains, rings and bracelets clinking softly against the metal.

"Goodnight Ty McCabe."

"Goodnight Never Ross."

I walk out of the gate and call a cab.

9

"*Bartleby, the Scrivener?*" Lacey asks with a wrinkled nose. "What's a scrivener?" I ignore her and try to focus on my paper. It's not something I want to write, and it's taking every ounce of strength I have to sit still. I'm afraid that if I look at her, I'll be more interested in the butterfly clip she has in her hair than I am about *A Story of Wall Street.* I yawn and slump back in my chair as I scroll through page after page of cliff notes.

"Hey Lacey," I say as she moves away from me and sits

down on the edge of her bed, a pair of nail clippers in one hand and a bottle of nail polish in the other. I try to keep my eyes on the computer, but they keep jumping around to the posters of half-naked girls that Lacey has put up on the wall behind her bed. "Have you ever had to write a paper that's longer than the story it's based on?"

"I'm majoring in biochem," she says as if that's explanation enough. I sigh and try not to imagine Lacey working in a laboratory of any kind. It's a scary thought. "Want to go to a movie with me tonight?" she asks randomly. I glance over at her and she smiles.

"With your girlfriend?" I ask, and she shakes her head.

"Nah," she says as she carefully applies a coat of bubblegum pink to her big toe. "I'm tired of playing games with my heart. I could use a dedicated friends only night, you know what I mean?" I stare at her for a moment. Roommate. Friend. Which one is she? Is she both now? I realize that the answer is yes. *When the hell did that happen?* The transition was too quick for me to see apparently, which is a scary thought. The more people I'm close to, the more people have an open shot at my heart. A feeling of discomfort creeps up on me as I try to figure out what to say.

"Uh, yeah, sure," I say as I give up and close my computer.

"Never?" Lacey asks, and I turn to find that she has tears in her eyes. They're dripping down her pretty face and landing on her bare feet. I stand up, but I'm not sure what to do; I don't even know what's wrong with her. When she looks up at me, I see that she's smiling through her sadness. "I never did say this, but … thank you."

"For what?" I ask as I move over and sit down next to her.

"For saving me," she says, and I notice that her hands are trembling just a bit. I reach down and take the nail polish gently from her fingers. "At the convenience store. If you hadn't, I … "

"Shush," I tell Lacey as I position her foot in my lap and take over the duty of painting her toenails. It's not something I do very often, so my careful strokes are about as neat as her shaking ones. Still, I think she appreciates it. As I paint, I start to cry, too, but not about the same thing. Lacey doesn't say anything which I appreciate, and we both shed our different feelings in the same way, taking quiet solace in one another's company.

Watching that stupid video must've opened something up inside of me because I miss my sisters so suddenly and so fiercely that it hurts inside. I remember my sister, Beth, painting my nails before my big performance, just days before I left her and everything else behind.

I know then that somehow, someway I'm going to have to open up the Pandora's box of my past soon. Sometimes, the only way to go forward, is to take a few, careful steps back.

Damn you, Ty McCabe. Damn you.

10

Ty shows up in the middle of my art history class.

The whole auditorium turns to look at him when he walks in and blinds us all with harsh, white winter sunshine. My professor stops talking and pauses between an image of Botticelli's *Primavera* and *The Birth of Venus.* Today's lecture is titled *Famous Artists of the Italian Renaissance* and as happy as I am to have a distraction from the admittedly dull lesson, I'm mortified when Ty waves at me and holds up his phone.

"Got your text," he says, like he's fucking oblivious that everyone is staring at him. The door slams shut and the room goes dark again, allowing the projector to once again display the slide show that all two hundred plus students have been studying for the past half hour. "You said it was urgent."I stand up, grab my backpack, and am grateful that I'm wearing boots today instead of heels, so that I can run up the steps and grab Ty by the arm.

"Let's go," I whisper as I open the door again and the class groans. Once it's shut behind us, I pull out a cigarette and search around for Ty's lighter. It's gone. He reaches into his own pocket and retrieves it, wiggling it teasingly in the air between us.

"I stole it back when you weren't paying attention," Ty says, and I can't figure out when that might have been. We've been hanging out on and off lately, always sporadically, never planned. We've gone for ice cream, seen a movie, even went to *the game,* which apparently means football. I've been going to the same university since I turned eighteen and got my GED and yet, I had no idea that we had a famous football team. Now all the sweatshirts I see with beavers on them make sense. *We don't give a dam about your team!* they say.

"Thanks for interrupting my lecture," I say as he bums a cigarette off me and puts it to his lips. "Now I'll probably fail the class. The professor already dislikes me because I disagree with some of his interpretations."

"Such as?" Ty asks as he lights up.

"The stupid fucking van Eyck painting with the couple and the dog, you know the one?" Ty raises his eyebrows and points at his own chest.

"Cashier, remember? Past work experience: whore. I don't know shit about paintings."

"Don't belittle yourself like that," I snap at him as I put the cigarette in my mouth and wait for a light. Ty pockets the lighter and leans forward, pressing the cherry of his cigarette against mine. Our faces are so close that for a moment, I forget to be mad at him. He has red and black piercings in his face today and a tight fitting wife beater draped over his chest. I take a few, quick, sharp inhales until the end of my Marlboro burns as orange as Ty's. "I hate when people do that."

"Fine," he says as we move away from the doors to the auditorium and up a steep slope towards the parking lot. "I won't say things like that if you tell me what this is all about." Ty holds out his phone so I can see the text message I sent to him.

I need to talk to you. Soon. It's important.

"You're the only person I know that uses correct grammar and punctuation in a text," he tells me as he puts his phone back in his pocket and blows smoke into the cool, moist air.

"And you're the only idiot I know that walks into a full lecture hall in the middle of class." Ty shrugs and lets the cigarette hang limply from his mouth.

"Then don't send me text messages like that. You had me worried."

"Worried?" I ask, and Ty gets pissed off all of a sudden. Without warning, he throws his cigarette to the ground and crushes it with his boot.

"Yeah, Never, worried. Is that such a fucking surprise to you?" I stop walking and just stare at him like he's crazy. Ty runs his fingers through his hair and holds out his hand like, *What the fuck are you waiting for, let's go!* I take a step back and watch as his dark eyes follow me.

"Don't talk to me like that," I tell him in a voice that's as cold as the breeze that ruffles my hair. *I was planning on telling you my secret. You can't talk to me that way.* "I am sick and fucking tired of people talking to me like that." Ty drops his hand and looks down, takes a deep breath and shakes his head.

"I'm sorry," he tells me, but I'm done for the day. I can't go back to class, so I turn away from Ty and head off in the direction of the dorms. "What did you need to talk to me about?" he asks as I stomp through pine needles and under the massive trees that help make up the natural beauty that our school is known for.

"Just forget it," I tell him as I pause at a crosswalk and adjust my backpack from one shoulder to the other. "It doesn't even matter. It's not important."

"Bullshit," Ty says, but his voice doesn't sound angry, it just sounds tired, and if I'm reading him correctly, *shameful.* Whatever his internal struggle is about, I don't want to know. This is why I don't get close to wounded guys. Guys like this, like Ty, they're just built to explode, to rain their burning past down on you and melt your soul. I should've kept my date with Rick. "Never … " I look over at Ty and paste an angry frown on my face.

"Go home and cool off. When you do, come find me. For now, fuck off." I start off across the road and pause on the other side when I hear Ty's voice sound out from behind me.

"You weren't planning on confessing your love for me or anything like that, were you?" he asks. And because I think it's a joke, I respond with, "Not in your wildest fucking dreams." I turn around to see what his face looks like because people like Ty flash everything they're feeling through their eyes like a slide show, when a bus passes between us, loud and obnoxious, spewing fumes into the clear air. When it's gone by and I finally have a clear view, Ty is nowhere to be seen.

11

I'm sitting in the lap of this guy who smells good and who seems nice, but that I can't stand listening to when he talks. Everything he says comes out with an explanation point at the end of it. *What are you majoring in?!* and *You have really beautiful hair!* I keep him quiet by pushing my tongue into his mouth, wrapping my arms around his neck and grinding my hips into his growing erection. Yeah, sure, somewhere inside of myself I know that I use sex as an escape, that even now I'm using this guy to forget about what happened between Ty and me yesterday, but I just don't know how else to deal.

"Whoa!" I hear a voice from behind me followed by bubbly giggles. It's Lacey.

"What?" I snap as I stare at her. She's dressed in this teeny tiny pink dress that crinkles and sparkles when she moves. Her legs are golden and long, lean and perfect. The perfect Barbie doll. There are guys hanging all over her, but she isn't interested in any of them.

"I was looking for you," she says with a laugh. I think she's plastered, but I'm not sure. I stand up, flicking away Exclamation Point Guy's hands as he grabs for me and clings to the fabric of the little black dress I chose tonight.

"Don't go!" he says, and I have to grit my teeth to keep from telling him to shut the fuck up.

"Keys," I say as Lacey pushes away a guy who won't stop kissing her neck. I hold out my hand and shake my palm for emphasis. "Now."

"Come on, Never. We want to go to the beach. That's why I was looking for you. Let's all go the beach together." Lacey holds up her arms and the entourage behind her cheers their consent.

"Keys," I repeat, unwilling to see Lacey perish in that stupid, little green car of hers. It would be both tragic and incredibly sad. She rolls her eyes and pouts her lips, but I don't take in any of it. "Keys."

"Fucking fine," she slurs as she reaches into her top and pulls them out. The blonde guy on her right groans and tries to lick the metal as she passes them over to me.

I shove his face back, grab Lacey by the chin and whisper, "Be careful." I kiss her on the cheek and send her on her way with her promise to keep her phone on. Bad things can happen at parties like this. Horrible things.

"Are you coming back to me?!" asks Exclamation Point

Guy. I close the door behind me and lean against it, letting my hair fall into my face, so that I can breathe for just a moment. I feel so jumbled and confused and messed up right now. I don't understand Ty any better than I understand myself. I thought he was making me better, but right now, I feel worse than ever. I put the base of my hand to my forehead, and slip my phone out of the inside pocket on my coat. Despite the fact that I'm wearing a sexy dress beneath it, I leave it on, like a layer of protection against the outside world.

No missed calls.

Fuck and damn it.

I put the phone away and lift up my head, putting a plastic smile on my face.

"Now where were we?" I ask the blonde guy with the nice chest and the pretty face. The guy who's so drunk that he's willing to do things he wouldn't normally do. The guy that I'll feel guilty about tomorrow. This isn't the type of man that I usually go for, not at all, but I feel like I need a break from those other kind, like I've got burn scars on my heart and body that haven't healed yet. I move across the room and swing my legs over the guy's knees. I unbutton his pants and try to ignore him when he talks.

"Are you going to blow me?" he asks. "I've never had a blow job before? Once, my girlfriend gave me a hand job though!" I pause with my hands on the waistband of his underwear. They're white briefs, not something I'm used to. The guys I fuck usually wear boxers.

"You have a girlfriend?" I ask and feel queasy inside. The blonde guy nods and tries to kiss me, but I turn my face away, unsure if I want to go through with this. I feel kind of … sick. With myself, with Ty, with this person, whoever he is.

"Yeah, we've dating for two years, ever since we started

going here. We met in a calc class!" he says as I lean back and wrinkle my nose. *What are you doing, Never? You haven't slept with anyone since that night you blew off your date with Rick. Are you seriously going to throw a whole month away like this? What do you think you're going to get out of this?*

"Look, uh," I pull my hands away from Exclamation Point Guy and fold them across my chest. "You, um, I can't do this." I shake my head and bite my lower lip hard enough that it bleeds. At least the pain wakes me up, tells me how stupid this really is. If I have a problem with Ty, I should call him. That's what a normal person would do. It's the only thing that makes any fucking sense.

As if summoned by my thoughts, my phone chirps at me, and I nearly fall off of the blonde dude's lap in my attempt to get it out of my pocket. There's a text. Just one. From Ty. My breath ceases to flow, and my heart doesn't pump.

hey Nevr sry i acted like a dick can u forgv me? i had a thng w sum grl. she trshed my place and i was pissed. no xcuses but i wanted u to know. call me.

I stare at the text for a moment.

"Come on," moans Exclamation Point Guy as he reaches down and frees himself from his pants. I give him a tight-lipped smile, put the phone away and pull out a piece of gum. I stuff it in my mouth, scoot forward, and fuck him.

All the while I know that I'm making a stupid, fucking mistake.

12

I leave Exclamation Point Guy passed out on a bed and walk out of that party with a smirk on my face, twirling the keys around my fingers like some kind of female Casanova. When I get outside and find Lacey making out with some girl that really should be wearing a bra but isn't, I retreat to her car and sit in the front seat with tears pouring down my face.

I sob and shake and scream. I grab the steering wheel with an iron grip and contract the muscles and tendons in my hand so hard that I feel like they're going to burst out of my skin and kill me. *I wish,* I think as I pull my phone out and dial Ty's number. I put it to my ear and sit in the dark silence of the car, trembling. I don't know what I'm going to say to him. What did he to do me anyway? Nothing. Nothing at all, and yet I'm so mad, I could spit. *Ty didn't make you fuck that guy, and he didn't break you. That wasn't him.*

"I'm not broken," I say aloud, but the only person I have to convince of that is me. Ty doesn't answer, and I don't leave a message because I don't know what to say to him. Suddenly, the loneliness of the car becomes stifling, and I have to climb out and walk back to the front yard where Lacey is lying on her back and looking up at the stars. She's holding hands with that girl, and they're both grinning like fools. "Let's go," I say to her, wondering when I stopped enjoying being alone.

"You take the car, Never," she says, eyes dewy and wide. "This is Trini's sorority house. She lives here."

"I'm an Alpha Omega," Trini says as the two girls turn towards one another and start to giggle. Lacey brushes Trini's dark hair away from her heart shaped face and they begin to kiss. I stare down at them for awhile, hoping they'll stop soon, but they don't. In fact, the longer I wait, the more intimate they get. Finally, I'm forced to retreat back to the little, green car by myself. It's a Fiesta, a gift from Lacey's dad. Wish I had a dad. Wish mine hadn't been murdered right in front of me. Wish I had someone to tell this secret, too.

I realize that I'm having a small anxiety attack and climb into the back seat for awhile to rest. As soon as my head hits the upholstery, I start to cry. Hours later, I fall asleep and spend the rest of my night in the back of Lacey's Ford, dreaming of one thing and one thing only.

Ty McCabe.

13

It's been almost three weeks since I last saw Ty, and I miss him so much it hurts when I move, like my muscles are sore from wishing too much. Why, I don't have any fucking clue. When I tell this to Lacey, she just smiles and gets all quiet. She's been acting strange ever since she met that girl, Trini. They hang out every available second of the day and even have these obnoxious sleepovers that make me want to grab my blankets and go curl up in the hallway. At least they don't have sex with me in the room. At least there's that.

"If you miss him so much, then call him," she tells me with a roll of her eyes, like this is a *duh* moment that I am just not getting. "I bet he'd be thrilled to hear from you." Lacey grabs her hair and twists it into a bun on the back of her head. As she does this, she watches me tack pictures to my wall. There are hundreds of them, and I'm determined to hang them all up. I've been working on this for days, plastering the wall next to my bed and planning to continue until I get to the closet. Lacey hasn't asked about them, but I saw her looking when she thought I was sleeping last night, using her phone as a flashlight.

"These are my sisters," I tell Lacey who raises her pale eyebrows. I've never told her about them. Not once. She only knows a little about my mom because she found my belly dancing costumes stuffed in the back of the closet. To assuage her curiosity, I had to tell her something. "Beth is the oldest." I pause and am royally pissed at myself for having to calculate my sister's age in my head. This is just something I should know without thinking. "I guess now she'd be about twenty-three." I point to a picture of a pretty girl with copper hair and a smile that could disarm even the toughest heart. Beth. God, it's hard to miss someone so much and hate them at the same time. It's a disconcerting feeling. "I'm next in the lineup." I move my finger across the wall like a pointer until I find a picture of me at sixteen. Lacey stands up and squeals.

"You were so cute!" she says as picks at the edge of the photo with her nails. They're painted bright yellow this week and while I find them obnoxious, I keep catching Trini sucking on them and telling Lacey how sexy they are. They're so goofy together that I have a sneaking suspicion that they think they're in love. I can't judge if they are or not; I'm not qualified, but if it's true, then I hope I never fall into it because when they're together, they act like idiots.

"Then there's Jade who's … " I count in my head again. "Twenty. Zella who's nineteen. India would be sixteen now, I guess." I sigh and try not to imagine my little sisters too clearly. The younger they were when I left, the more I miss them, the less culpable I hold them for what happened. Beth, Jade, and Zella are at least half responsible for me leaving. "Lettie is thirteen and Lorri is ten." I point them all out, a sea of girls with pretty lips, pale skin, and eyes that sparkle with blue and green flecks. We all look like our mother, like a sea of copper haired clones. Except for Beth, Zella, and me, nobody shares the same father. My mom's as big a whore as I am.

I drop the pictures to my bed and they flutter down to the red and black comforter like a swarm of butterflies.

Tears are falling again, and I don't know why. I don't know anything anymore. I thought I had things figured out, at least a little bit. Stay busy, find a reason to live in the morning, cry myself to sleep at night. I didn't have friends, and I brushed bodies with bruised souls. Now I can't even stomach the thought of sex and being alone makes me physically ill.

Ty has changed me; Lacey has changed me; I'm changing myself. Just everything's changing, and I don't know how to deal. It's happening fast, too fast for me to follow. I don't like it. I don't feel in control now. The world is spinning, and I can't stop it, no matter how hard I try.

"Hey," Lacey says as she scoops the photos into a neat stack and sets them on the edge of her desk. "Why don't I blow off my date with Trini tonight, and we'll go out, just me and you. No boys, no girls, just a round of mini golf?"

I open my mouth to tell her how incredible that sounds when there's a knock at the door.

"Just a sec," Lacey says as she touches my arm with her

hand. "It's probably just Trini." She moves to the door and opens it without bothering to ask who's there. Shame 'cause who's there is Ty.

He's standing in the hallway with a blue T-shirt, a face full of silver piercings and a pair of black jeans tucked into his black boots. The laces aren't just undone on these, they're missing entirely. His hair is free of products and hangs softly around his dark eyes and over his ears. His face looks strained, like maybe he hasn't had such an easy couple of weeks.

Good, I think as I grab my coat off the back of my chair.

"We're kind of on our way out," I say with a tight-lipped smile. I search my pockets for gum and find some, stuffing it into my mouth, so I don't have to talk anymore than is absolutely necessary. Lacey looks between Ty and me, and with a grimace, steps aside to let him in. I give her a look that asks, *What the fuck are you doing?*

She cringes and grabs her own jacket off of a hook near the door, mouthing *Sorry* to me as she goes. When she gets back, I'm going to ring her neck.

I throw my coat onto the bed and cross my arms over my chest.

Ty is just standing there with his dark gaze trained on my face and a gentle frown tracing the sexy curve of his lips.

"What do you want?"

"Never … "

"Don't stand there and sputter," I say. "Cut to the fucking chase, Ty, or get out." He doesn't seem taken aback my anger. In fact, he drops his chin a bit like he expected me to act this way.

"What did you want to talk to me about that day?" I roll my eyes to the ceiling and count to three.

"I don't know, Ty," I lie. "I don't even remember anymore,

what do you care? You don't even know me." Ty shifts his feet slightly and looks up. The strain in his face is giving way to anger. We're both upset and neither of us knows why. We don't know how to read our own emotions, so reading each other's is virtually impossible.

"Are you pissed because I fucked some girl?" he asks as he glances over at the wall behind my bed, gets lost in the collage of my history. Ty takes a step forward, but I move in front of him, determined to keep him out of my past.

"Are you pissed because I fucked some boy?" I ask and Ty switches his gaze back to my face.

"Let's not go there, Never," he says, but he sounds pissed. I like that. I feel disgusting because of it, but I do. I like that he's pissed. Let him be. Let him get raging fucking psychotically mad at me. I want to see that emotion from him right here, right now.

"That's right," I tell him as I drop my hands to my sides and take a step closer. "I was in the middle of fucking someone when I got your message. I read it while his cock slid in and out of me, is that the place you don't want to go?"

"That's your business." Ty says this, but he doesn't mean it. It's bothering him. I know because he starts to pace the room, running a hand through his hair and chewing on his lip ring. "I didn't seek someone out to have sex with, you know," he tells me, like that's supposed to mean something.

"Okay," I say as I watch him carefully. I don't want him to look at my photos; I don't want him to even glance that way. "They came to you, right? They must've paid nicely. How much? A hundred bucks? Two?" Ty stops walking and spins around, gets real close to my face and glares daggers at me.

"I'm lost, Never," he says, and his voice is so soft that I almost break, almost give into him and forget this ever happened, but I can't. I feel betrayed. I wanted to tell him my secret and he wanted to do what he's always done and go bury his feelings between some girl's thighs. Obviously our friendship meant nothing to him or he wouldn't have done that. I didn't. Not until he practically forced me into a corner. "I just … I was afraid, Never."

"Of what?" I ask. "Not being able to pay rent?"

"Having my heart broken," he says, and I feel these walls come crashing down around me. Walls that I've spent years building back up. My breath gets caught in my throat, and tears prick my eyes like needles. I don't acknowledge his words or what they might mean. Instead, I pretend that I don't even hear him.

I stand there in silence while he waits for me to say something. I can see in his eyes that he's desperate to get past this darkness in his life, to step forward into the light and do things differently, but he needs help and I am in no place to give it.

"Get out," I whisper as I realize my hands are shaking again. "Get out and leave me alone. My life is complicated enough without you around." Ty makes a noise in his throat, just a soft, small noise, like a whimper. "Get out," I say again, but my voice is trembling. "You're too broken for me to fix." Ty looks up suddenly and his eyes burn hot. Without warning, he moves forward, and I have to crane my neck back to look up at him.

"Never," Ty says, and we both lose a battle that was worth fighting, give into old habits and stay shrouded in blackness.

14

Ty and I brush our lips across one another, but we don't touch, instead we just breathe on each other's skin, basting our aching flesh with hot breath that comes out in short little bursts while we pant away and try not to press our bodies together. It's hard though for two people that have always relied on sex to solve their problems any other way. From loneliness to financial hardship to boredom, there it was, this easy thing that we could do to soothe our aches temporarily. Little did we know that each time we betrayed who we were inside, we were cutting ourselves, just a nick here, a nick there. Now we're both so covered in one another's blood that it's impossible to escape.

Ty doesn't kiss me, but he does drag his hands down my sides, getting his fingers caught in the fabric of my sweater, the pleats of my skirt. I groan and try to reach down to grab his wrists, to stop him, to push him away, but his arms come up instead, snatch mine and slam them over my head. A picture of Lacey's mother falls to the floor and the glass inside it shatters. Neither Ty or I notice.

"I'm done playing games with you," Ty tells me, but I have no fucking clue what he's talking about. If anyone's playing games, it's him. "This is what you want, isn't it?" I don't know what to say with his mouth hovering over my lips. His hand squeezing my wrists so hard it's painful. His fingers dipping down, down, down, lower. No? Is that what I'm supposed to say? Yes? Yes? No?

Ty brushes my clit with his thumb but just barely, just enough that I can feel it, that I arch my hips forward for more, but not enough that I get any relief out of it. Instead, I sag against the wall, let him use all of the strength in that gently sweeping bicep to hold me there. He's got sweat on the tip of his nose, across his forehead, and down the sides of his neck. I wish I could take his shirt off, explore that hard plane of flesh, finally get a chance to explore a man's body like I never have before.

But I know Ty's type; I knew it the first moment I laid eyes on him.

Ty isn't the guy that takes you to bed and touches your clit with gentle fingers, that whispers sweet nothings in your ear, that lubes up his cock before he slides into you.

Rick was one of those guys maybe but not Ty. I've known

it all along anyway.

"Fuck you," I say, but the words are half spit because I can't enunciate properly, not with this need bubbling up so hot and strong inside of me. There's a misunderstanding here, a big one, and if we don't clear it up, we'll just be making the same mistake, over and over and over again.

Ty looks me right in the face with those dark eyes, smirks at me with those sexy lips, and runs his tongue across them as if he knows how to push every button on my body with a simple look. He unbuttons his pants and puts a hand under my ass. With considerable strength, Ty lifts me up and thrusts into me at the same time.

There's this vicious blending of bodies and strong wills and stubborn characters and for a split second, there's no *you* and no *me*, just *us*. It fades away as quickly as it came and soon we're back to just being human; two grunting, sweating, moaning souls grinding together for whatever reason is important *today*, filling whatever need has to be filled *now*. I don't think for awhile, and if Ty tells you that he does, he's lying. He keeps his hand on my wrists, keeps me pinned there while he slides into me with long, hard strokes, tries to bury whatever problems he has in me while I let him fill the empty hole inside of myself.

That's not to say that the sex isn't good. Oh god, it's good. It's explosive and wild and everything I've always craved. Ty is hot and sexy and perfect, but suddenly, I get this image in my head of him taking money from me. I think about handing him a wad of cash and getting this very same thing, feeling his hand squeezing the flesh on my ass, the movement of his cock inside of me.

"Stop it," I say as I squeeze my eyes shut and try to push the thought from my head. Ty drops my hands suddenly, pulls away from me as my feet the hit the floor. I crumple to the ground with my hands over my head. Without knowing why, I'm sobbing. For me, for Ty, I'm not sure. When he tries to take a step towards me, I scream at him. "Get out!" I shout as I fly to my feet. I hit Ty in the chest with a fist. "Get out! Get out! Get out!" He fixes his pants, gives me one last terrified look and leaves the room, slamming the door behind him.

15

There's a zombie cupcake sitting on my bedside table. It has a purple wrapper and white frosting with a green face piped onto the middle of it, tongue lolling out to the side, red gel icing dripping like blood from its empty eye socket.

"What the hell is this?" I ask Lacey who's sitting up in bed, working her comb through her pretty, blonde hair. She isn't very careful about it and I cringe as I hear strands snapping with each stroke. With one last yank, she sets the blue brush down on the bed next to her and curls her hands over her knees.

"That's for you," she says, grinning and flashing me the skinny gap between her two front teeth. I knock the cupcake to the floor and roll over with a groan. Lacey's there in an instant, grabbing my shoulder and shaking me like she's not a hundred percent certain that I'm still alive.

"Come on, Never! You've been a zombie for days. What the hell is wrong with you?" I ignore her and stare at the wall beside my bed. There are black marks there that I drew with eyeliner. One for each day since I kicked Ty out, seven in total. I reach out a hand and smear them across the textured wall so that they look like soot. Lacey sighs and bends down, presumably to grab the cupcake. "And here I was, thinking that you were on your way to being cured."

"Cured?" I ask as I look over my shoulder at her. She's adjusting her pearly pink sweater with her long, yellow nails, positioning it just right so that it frames the small swell of cleavage she's managed to dredge up with a push up bra. Unfortunately, the sweater is a perfect match to her lipstick. It's too pale and makes her look washed out, but I don't say anything about it. I'm too curious about her previous statement.

"Yeah," she says, not getting how important her words are to me. They might not mean anything, but they might mean everything, too. I have to hear someone else say it. I just have to. "Ever since you started hanging out with Ty, you've been … I don't know, thawed out or something."

"Are you calling me frigid?" I ask, voice stiff and kind of scary. Lacey stops fidgeting with her outfit and meets my eyes. She looks tentative now, though, like she might retract her previous statement. I admit, I can be kind of scary sometimes. "Sorry, I know you didn't mean that." Lacey sighs again and hands me the cupcake. Miraculously, even though it's taken a fall, it looks, for the most part, unscathed. My breath catches in my throat.

"I just meant that when we first met, you were kind of … I don't know … cold? Like you didn't care about anything." Lacey shrugs her shoulders. "Lately you've been … normal?" she asks this like a question. I stare at her for a long moment that stretches uncomfortably between us while Lacey fidgets and looks at anything and everything but me.

"Normal?" I ask her and she jumps in surprise.

"God, Nev," she says, giving me a nickname. It's something I haven't had in years. Despite everything, I smile. "Don't scare me like that," she says, noticing my smile and relaxing a bit. Lacey stands up and pulls my blankets off of me. "Yes, normal. You know, I didn't even know you *had* sisters let alone their names. Then all of a sudden, you've got these pictures and this smile, and you're just a different person. I wasn't sure what it was at first, but when I saw you at the game with him, I figured it out."

"Figured what out?" I ask, sitting up and watching Lacey move across the room to my dresser. She opens the top drawer, extracts a lacy, black bra and tosses it to me. I take it and clutch it to my chest while I wait for her to answer me.

"That you're good for each other," she replies as she nibbles at her lip and picks through my shirts with her fingernails. When she finds one she likes, she pulls it out and throws it over the back of my computer chair.

"We're not a couple," I protest as I swing my feet out of bed. I stand up and check my phone, but there aren't any messages. Rather than discouraging me, it puts this fire under my ass, this itch to get out, to get going. I don't quite understand it, but I want to roll with it, see where it takes me. Isn't it amazing how one, nice comment can change your outlook on something? Or maybe I'm just tired of being depressed. Seven days is a long time to lay comatose and feel sorry for oneself.

"You don't have to be a couple," says Lacey as she hands me a pair of dark wash jeans to go with my red tank top. "You get each other, isn't that enough?"

I grab the pants, dress in record time, and ask one, final question.

"Can you drive me?"

16

Lacey drops me off next to the gatehouse at Ty's apartment complex.

The guy working the morning shift is sympathetic, but tells me he can't let me in without permission from one of the residents.

"I could give him a call?" the man asks as I run my hand through my hair and try not to pace. I don't know why I'm so nervous. Ty might not even be home. Besides, I should've called fist. I don't even know why I'm here. Suddenly, I get this panicked feeling in my chest; my heart's fluttering like a butterfly, battering my insides and making me feel sick.

"Yeah, sure, okay, call him," I say as I sit down on the edge of the curb and put my face in my hands. What if he tells the guy to tell me to fuck off? What will I do then? I look up suddenly and glance over my shoulder. The guard has just started to dial the numbers. It's not too late to stop him. "Wait!" I say as I stand up. The man pauses and looks at me strangely through the pass-through window. "Um, I bet he's not even home. Don't worry about it. I'll call him later." I start to turn away when a familiar voice sends chills down my spine.

"Liar," Ty says from behind me. I spin around to see him coming through a small gate next to the security office. He smiles at the guard and pauses just a few feet in front of me. He looks really … good. I find myself tongue-tied as I try to figure out what to say. Actually caring about someone I've slept with is a new thing for me. I'm not used to having to deal with the feelings that sex can bring out in a person because I don't stick around long enough to have them. I swallow hard and take in Ty's ripped jeans, his brown boots, the black T-shirt that only emphasizes the flatness of his chest and belly.

"Liar?" I ask because I don't know what else to say. Ty licks his lip and plays with his lip ring, a sign that he's thinking really hard about what to say next. I don't like that; I don't like that at all. He has a red jacket tossed over his shoulder and his hair is perfectly arranged. It kind of looks like he's getting ready for a date. I blurt out my thoughts and cringe. "Got a hot date?"

Ty laughs, but it's a little bitter, a tad cynical.

"You never call," he tells me as I cross my arms over my chest and shiver at the icy breeze. *Tank tops in winter; I must be a true California girl.* "That's why I called you a liar."

"It goes both ways, McCabe," I say as I shift back and forth between my feet and pretend that I don't notice that the guard is eavesdropping on us. "You could've called me, too." Ty looks down at the cement for a moment, and I get this terrible feeling that he's going to tell me to get lost. Neither of us asked for this relationship, whatever it might be. Maybe neither of us was ready for this?

Then he looks up and tosses me his coat.

"Here, put this on," Ty says as he pulls a cigarette out of his pants and lights up. "You're going to need it. We have a long walk ahead of us." He smiles and gives me a once over with one eyebrow raised in amusement. "Hope you didn't walk all the way down here in that top?" he asks this as a question as I slip my arms into his fleece lined coat and bum a cigarette out of the front pocket. Ty hands me the lighter as I put it between my lips.

"Lacey drove me," I say as he steps forward and my heart skips a beat. *Are we even going to talk about what happened?* I wonder as Ty reaches out and grabs the zipper on the coat. He pulls it up all the way up to my chin and smiles. I kind of hope he just ignores what happened between us, that he and I can just pretend that we never slept together. Apparently, he feels the same way, but he's got a whole different set of torture ready for me. While I've been wasting away in bed and watching daytime television, Ty's been picking up the pieces of his life and arranging them together just so.

"Good. I'd feel awfully guilty if I knew you'd frozen your ass off for this, but I'm glad you're here because honestly, I was on my way over to get you." Now it's my turn to raise my eyebrows.

"Huh?" I ask as I pocket the lighter and fall into step beside

Ty. He's heading in the direction of the university and walking briskly enough that I can make an educated guess about where he's going. "You have an appointment?" I ask, and he nods. There's this little, pesky smile on his face that I'm not sure about. "Job interview?" But then, why would he have been on his way to get me for a job interview? That doesn't make any sense.

"Nope," Ty says as he lets the cigarette hang from his mouth while he fishes in his back pocket for something. "Better. Keep guessing and maybe I'll tell you."

"This is stupid," I tell him, but I watch his hand emerge with a brochure and find that my curiosity is piqued. He holds it out to the side with one hand and pulls his cigarette from his mouth with the other.

"Guess," he says again as he blows smoke into the wind. It catches in the air and swirls around me, enhancing the smell of the coat which already stinks like tobacco. Maybe it would bother some people but for whatever reason, I find it comforting. I roll my eyes like Lacey.

"Um, we're going to another game?" Ty wrinkles his nose.

"No, do you really want to?" I can't help but laugh, but as soon as the amusement dies down, I'm glaring at him.

"I fucking hate surprises," I say and Ty hands me the brochure with a sigh.

Student Health Services, it says.

"Um, okay?" I say as I hand it back to him. He takes it and turns it over. In blue pen, there's a simple schedule written out. *Noon-thirty: Me. One: Never.* He shows me this, too. "You do know that SHS is for students only." Ty nods and tucks the brochure into the front pocket of my coat.

"I know," he says, and this time, the smile on his face is so genuine that it highlights his dimples and his perfect cheeks and makes his eyes look a million times brighter. His spine is straight and he's walking with a pep in his step.

"You didn't?" I ask because my guess can't possibly be right. "You got into the U?" Ty's face just explodes into this massive grin and suddenly he's hugging me, wrapping his warm arms around my waist and swinging me in a circle. When he sets me down, this fount of laughter just bubbles from his throat. "How? It takes weeks, months for them to approve an application."

"I know," he says as he takes my hand and doesn't let go. We keep walking. "I filled it out right after I met you. I filled out the *federal application for student aid,* too," he says with a wink. "The FAFSA. Plus, I got a scholarship through the housing authority program, so I'm covered for next semester, Never. I'm in."

"I'm super proud of you, Ty," I say as we pause at a street corner and dump both of our cigarettes into the nearby ashtray. "Really, I am." I look up and see that he's staring at me with a strange expression on his face like there's more. I make an incorrect assumption about his look and blurt out, "About what happened … before … I … "

"Never," Ty says as he touches a finger to my chin and pulls my gaze from his butterfly tattoos and up to his face. "Listen to me. You and I, we both have problems." I push his hand away and look down at the cement. The wind is blowing my hair into my face, obscuring my vision with ebony and crimson. Ty sweeps it away from my eyes with his ringed fingers. He's wearing mostly pearls today which is strange. Every other time I've seen him, he's had a myriad of different gems in all sorts of colors.

"Thank you, Captain Fucking Obvious," I say because standing here on this street corner with Ty McCabe, I feel exposed, like I'm naked on the top of a mountain, revealed for the world to see. I don't like it. Not one little bit.

"What if I said we could help each other through those problems?" I stare into his eyes and wait for the other shoe to drop.

"Okay?" I say, and I sound sarcastic and bitter and completely unpleasant. I close my eyes and force myself to take a calming breath. Ty is trying here, so I owe it to him to try, too. I open my eyes and notice that he's shivering. I realize how cold my face and hands are and immediately wrap my arms around him. *He did give me his coat after all.* "How?"

"You know how alcoholics have sponsors?" he asks me, and I don't really like the analogy.

"Sure, yeah."

"Well, that's what we're going to be."

"Sponsors?"

"Yep."

"But neither of us are alcoholics," I say as I step back. The light has changed and we've finally got an opportunity to cross the street. "You want to like, go to an AA meeting or something?"

"No," Ty says as he grabs my hand again and pulls me through the crosswalk. "I want to go to an SAA meeting."

"SAA?" I ask as we head towards the hill and the massive white and beige buildings of the campus. "What the hell is that?"

"Sex Addicts Anonymous," Ty says simply and my heart jumps into my throat.

Oh. Shit.

I dig my heels into the pavement and refuse to take another step.

"There's no way in hell I'm going to one of those meetings," I protest, and I feel hot and jittery, like there are ants marching over my skin and making me itch. I shake my head and turn away from Ty so that I'm facing the inside of a sub shop. There aren't any people inside at the moment, and two of the employees are lip-locked behind the counter. It's not a pleasant sight, so I switch my gaze to the sidewalk.

"Never, we need this. Both of us. Or at least, I need it, and I need you to help me." I shake my head. I am not capable of helping anyone with anything.

"I can't, Ty," I say. I'm panicking right now and deep down, I know why. It's because he's right. He's right. He is so fucking right that I can't stand it. I should've gone out with Rick, hit the straight and narrow, got married and had babies. That's what I should've done, but here I am, standing with Ty McCabe on a street corner talking about sex addiction. How perfect is that? Somehow, even though I can't admit it to myself at the moment, I think that I'm right where I need to be. How fucked up is that? "I can't do this right now," I whisper even though I know I will. I will do it.

"That's okay," Ty says as he steps up real close to me and lights a cigarette next to my ear. When he exhales, I inhale and try to find some modicum of peace when the smoke fills my lungs. "You don't have to go right away. The meeting isn't until later. Right now, you and I have something else to do."

"And what's that?" I ask because I can't handle the suspense.

"You and I are going to get tested."

17

I'm sitting in a plastic chair next to Ty, and I'm shaking so bad that my teeth are chattering. It's not that I'm cold, not with Ty's jacket wrapped around me like a second skin. I'm shaking because sitting here in this office with these posters all around me, I feel sick.

Do you feel alone? Do you use sex as a way to connect with strangers? Have your desires motivated you to seek sex with people you wouldn't normally choose? How about in places or situations you wouldn't normally choose? Do your sexual encounters leave you at risk for STIs, unwanted pregnancies, rape or violence? Have you ever had a sexual encounter that has left you feeling hopeless or alienated? Suicidal?

Everywhere I fucking look there's another poster with a girl or a boy who's either crying or holding their head like they're in pain. And my answer to every single fucking question that's printed above their melancholy faces is YES. Y. E. S. It's almost enough to make me walk out. The only thing keeping me seated is Ty's hand in my lap. He's been letting me examine his tattoos as a way to keep my mind occupied.

"So I only got things with wings," Ty says as I trace an orange and black butterfly on the back of his hand. "Because I wanted to be free. Every time I got a new tattoo, I promised myself that this was the day I changed everything. This was the day I grew my own wings and flew away."

"What happened?" I whisper, afraid that if I speak too loudly, the receptionist might look up and see me for what I really am. A person with a broken soul. I swallow hard and glance at the door fearfully when the bell above the entrance rings. There are no other patients in here now, but if there were, I don't think I could do this. I couldn't sit here with anyone who knows what I really am, what's wrong with me, why I'm here. Except for Ty. Just Ty. Fortunately, it's just a delivery man. He drops a small package at the front desk and leaves while I keep my head tilted down and away for fear that he'll memorize my face, call me out on the street or something, see me in class.

"I never really tried, Never. I didn't know what to try for."

"But you do now?" I ask, but before Ty can answer, the door to the back opens.

"Mr. McCabe?" the woman with the clipboard says. She's

smiley and nice and all, but I bet underneath all of that sweet, she's thinking, *What the hell is wrong with these kids? Why are they here? What happened to make them this way?* I stare into her brown eyes and am paralyzed with fear. This is my worst nightmare come true. Inside these walls, I cannot lie. I cannot pretend, not anymore.

"Are you going to be okay?" Ty asks me as he shakes my knee gently to grab my attention. I look over at him and don't know what to say. No? Is that an option.

"I have to tell you a secret," I say to him. Maybe now isn't the best time, but after. I'll tell him after. "When we get out of here. I want to tell you what I didn't say that day you picked me up in Art History." Ty nods his head and presses a chaste kiss to my cheek.

"I would like that, Never," he says to me. "I really would." As he rises to his feet, I have to close my eyes to keep myself from following after him. I count up to a hundred and back down to one again. When I open my eyes, there are tears in them.

Here in this office, in this room with the too true posters, my own mortality sits in a plastic chair of her own, stares me straight in the face and smirks. I feel her eyes on me, calculating, judging, disapproving.

"I already know what you think of me," I say aloud and notice that the receptionist's eyes lift from her computer for just a second and gaze out at me. I give her a tight-lipped smile and resist the urge to flip her off. My anger is just a reaction to the fear I have inside of myself, a fear that somehow, one of the dozens of stupid mistakes I've made, the desperate attempts at filling that deep, aching, loneliness, will kill me. That I'll go out of this world alone and without dignity. That I'll never really understand what it means to live.

I get up three times and go to the door, and three times, I

turn around and go back, sit in that plastic chair and wait with my inner Never staring at me, waiting for judgment day. I don't read any of the magazines that sit on the table to my right nor do I watch the silent TV screen that's hanging near the ceiling, flashing bright colors at me in a blurry slide show. I just sit and wait and think. And when I've had enough of that, I get out my phone and dial a number that I haven't dialed in a long, long time.

Three rings later, and I hear: "Hello?"

I swallow hard, try not to cry again and say one word, "Beth?"

18

"Never? Oh my god, Mom, it's Never. Never?" I open my mouth to speak, but the words won't come out. They're stuck deep down inside, buried by hurt and pain. I start to cry again and dash the tears away angrily while I listen to my sister's frantic voice. "Never, are you still there? Please answer me, Never." Beth is hysterical. She's sobbing, and I can just imagine her face in my head, the way her nose turns red when she cries and the way her pretty eyes go all bloodshot like she's been smoking pot or something. I always thought she was prettiest like that though, raw and not so perfect as she pretends to be. I miss her, and I hate her.

"Why?" I ask that one single word, and Beth goes silent. People are shouting in the background. I don't know which people, my sisters or maybe even my mom, but I'm definitely not ready to talk to her yet. I don't even know why I called. After five years, I just up and do it in the middle of a fucking clinic? Is it Ty? Is it me? What is it? Maybe it's because I know that I'm here for a reason, Ty brought me here for a reason, and if it's to find out that I've got something, that I'm going to die, I need to get this off of my chest or my spirit really will just disintegrate and become nothing. I swallow my anger at Beth for just a moment. "Why didn't you stand up for me when you knew I was right?" Beth stays silent, and I watch the clock across the room from me, hanging over the other Never's head like a halo.

Ticktock, she says.

"Oh, Never, where are you? Are you safe?" she blurts out.

The door across the room opens and Ty emerges with a small bandage on his elbow. When he first steps out, he's smiling, but as soon as he sees my face, he practically runs across the office and kneels down beside me. I look at him looking up at me.

"Are you okay?" he asks again, and I can see he's worried that bringing me here was a mistake. What he doesn't know is that this day, this blip in the reel of life events that will inevitably define who and why and how and what Never Ross and Ty McCabe are, is the most important day of all, the turning point for both of us. That's why it's hard; it has to be hard or it wouldn't count. That's the rule of the universe, I suppose. As Andrew Carnegie once said, *Anything in life worth having is worth working for!*

I don't respond to Ty's question because I'm not sure of the answer.

"Never? Never? Answer me, please, god," Beth sobs as Ty pulls the phone from my stiff fingers, looks at the screen and then puts it to his ear.

"She's having a crisis of character at the moment," Ty says as he gives me the world's smallest, cutest smile. "I'll have her call you back." He hangs up, and then slips the phone into the front packet of the coat. "This is your secret?" he asks, and he sounds awfully broken up about it. Ty moves from the floor and sits on the chair next to me, taking my hand in his and weaving his ringed fingers through mine.

"Part of it," I admit as the door in the back opens once again and reveals the smiley lady with the ponytail and the perfect teeth.

"Never Ross?"

I close my eyes and gather courage around myself, all of it that I can muster. I have that in spades, you know. It takes a lot of courage to go through life in the dark. Most people have a nightlight, something to chase away the monsters and beautify the storm, but I've never had that, so I've learned to be brave. I might fuck strange people and I might cry and maybe I smoke too much, but I know how to deal, so that's what I'm going to do.

"Never," Ty whispers so close to my ear that I can feel his hot breath against my skin. In spite of the situation, it makes me shiver. "It's your turn."

I open up my eyes and rise to my feet. All the while my hands are shaking, and the mortal me still sits beneath a plastic clock in a plastic chair and smiles.

19

I cry through my entire examination.

I cry when they ask me routine questions.

When was your last sexual encounter? Who was your last sexual partner? How many sexual partners have you had in your lifetime? Do you use protection?

I cry when they take my weight and my height and my blood pressure.

Five foot seven, one hundred and forty-one pounds, the

perfect 120/80.

I cry when they ask me to remove my jacket.

It smells like cigarettes and dangerous boys with broken hearts, like a shield against painful reality.

When I first start to cry, the woman who's asking the questions feels really bad and even gives me a hug and a cup of black coffee. I sip it down slowly, but it doesn't help. I just have to let the emotions wash over me and feel them, all of them. Hiding away from them doesn't work. Hiding away from them is what got me here.

They poke my arm and draw blood, lots of it. When they first put the needle into my flesh, the pain is almost unbearable, like a laughable analogy of all the pricks I've used in myself to try and cover up my feelings. I bite my tongue and force myself to watch the nurse weave the metal into my flesh. She wiggles it around for a moment, and then tugs on the plunger at the end of the tube.

"Okay, Never, try to sit still and we'll get this over with as quick as we can." Crimson fills the tube, glistening bright under the fluorescent lights as it's pulled from my body, bit by painful bit. "We have to get a few samples since there are multiple tests. You did say you wanted a full workup, didn't you?"

"Test me for all of it," I tell her without any sort of inflection. The tears have finally dried on my face, salty and sticky. Now I feel a bit emotionless like I'm in shock or something. "I'm probably disease ridden." The nurse laughs, but I can tell she's only doing it out of nervousness. Once the tube is full, she pulls it off the needle and slips it into a tray of rounded slots. There's at least a dozen of them, so I know I'm in for the long haul. I lean my head back against the chair and watch as she repeats the process.

"I know it doesn't seem like much, but your boyfriend must

care a lot about you," she says, and I don't correct her assumption that Ty is my boyfriend. She knows that he was the last person I slept with and I'm guessing by his actions that I'm the same for him, so it makes sense. I wish it was that simple. *Plunge, blood, twist, slot, repeat.*

"Because it's romantic to find out if your lover is as diseased as you are?" I ask, and am sorry that I even said it.

"A lot of men refuse to come in here. We get more girls than we do boys, most of them saying that their lovers want *them* to get tested, but won't get tested themselves. It makes me sick." The nurse smiles at me and searches my face for a moment before she looks back down at the bloody tube in her hand. "I understand that it's only been a week since your last sexual encounter, but did you want us to run a pregnancy test as well?"

"Lay it all on me," I tell her.

Either she takes this literally or Ty signed me up in advance for this torture because their next course of action is to hand me a water bottle and a cup, assign me to a bathroom and force me to pee.

I sit on the toilet with my pants around my ankles and just stare at the back of the door. I've left the lights off, but I can still see the poster. There's a girl who looks a lot like me with almond shaped eyes, curved brows, and a crooked smile. She even has a nose like mine. It's small and pointy, a feature of mine that I've always hated but that guys often tell me is cute. She's holding a sign that says, *I Am Worth It.*

"I'll bet you are," I say to her as I sigh and try to force myself to go into the stupid cup. If I ever get horny again after this, it'll be a miracle. I should've stuck with Rick's road to redemption because Ty's is rocky and filled with thorns. Ty. Ty McCabe. The mysterious man with the sexy smirk and the perfect abs and the bleeding heart. What a fucking nightmare. What am I going to do with him anyway? Why did I even go back to his apartment? To be friends again? Is that what I want to be? Do I have to define our relationship?

You get each other, isn't that enough?

I shake my head, down the water bottle, and do what I need to do. When I'm finished, I wash my hands and put the lid on the cup, taping it down just so as I've been instructed. When I come out of the bathroom, blinking my eyes at the bright light, the nurse takes it with a smile and a gleeful *Thank you!* that I just don't buy because really, all I gave her was piss. I put my hands on my hips.

"Am I done now?" I ask as I look around for my coat.

"If you're looking for your jacket, I gave it back to Mr. McCabe," she says with a smile. "And no, darling, you're not quite done yet, there is one more test. We need to get a swab. Come with me and I'll show you to your room." I sigh and follow her out, watch as she hands my piss to another lab tech, removes her gloves, and washes her hands with foamy soap. She then escorts me to another room, a much scarier room.

There are pregnant women and women with babies plastered on all the walls, and in the center of this white washed hell hole is a chair with metal stirrups and straps that look so medieval that I nearly bolt in fear. The nurse puts a hand on my arm as if to comfort me.

"There's a hospital gown there for you. If you wouldn't mind putting it on, we can get started. You can leave your top on, but please remove your pants and underwear. The doctor will be with you shortly."

"What if I do mind?" I ask as I give the nurse a look over my left shoulder. "What the fuck is this?" Miss Smiley does what she does best, putting on this big, goofy grin that's supposed to make me feel better but doesn't.

"We need to get a vaginal swab to make sure we can thoroughly rule out the possibility of infection, Miss Ross. With your sexual history, it's – "

"Fine," I say as I hold up my hands. I don't need to hear anymore about it. I just need to get this over with before I lose my nerve. "That's fine." The nurse squeezes my shoulder and leaves me alone with smiling stock photos. I don't bother to use the bathroom and instead just strip right there in the office, feeling horribly vulnerable and more uncomfortable than ever.

What's the difference? Removing your panties for the doctor or for some guy you don't even know? Since when do you care so much, Never?

And then I'm holding my lacy boyshorts in my hand and crying again. I press them to my face which sounds weird but isn't because I think I'm starting to realize exactly what it is that's wrong with me.

Never Ross wants to be loved.

It's that simple, but it's not that easy.

20

“I oughta fucking kill you for making me go through that shit,” I tell Ty as I light up just steps from the clinic's front door. My hands are shaking so bad that it takes me four tries to get a flame out of the friggin' lighter. I blame it on the trauma of the experience combined with the horrible two week wait that I am now being forced to endure. I can't get the results soon enough. Until then, I'll be lucky if I can sleep, eat, or manage to pass my midterms. "They spread me open like a Thanksgiving turkey." Ty laughs and tries to take the cigarette from my outstretched hand, but I pull it away and give him a *look.*

"At least you didn't have an intern grab your dick and shove a Q-tip into it," he says, and it's my turn to laugh. It's a nervous laugh, but at least it's there. I feel lighter somehow, like I left all my baggage at the clinic with no return address. *Please do not return to sender,* I think as Ty grabs me by the waist with one hand, pulls me against his chest, and steals the cigarette from me with the other. He releases me as he puts it to his lips and smiles. "That swab thing is now on my 'Weirdest Shit I've Ever Done' list."

"At least you didn't have to put your legs in metal stirrups and have some uptight bitch put a spotlight on your crotch. It was like some kind of science fiction book gone wrong. Ugh."

"Mine was worse," Ty promises as we meander through the campus without any specific sense of direction. "When they made me take my pants off, I was hard."

"Why?" I ask which is a fucking stupid question.

"Because I was thinking of you," Ty says, and I roll my eyes.

"I'm immune to one-liners, McCabe. I think you should know that by now. I resisted the one you fed me when we first met, didn't I?" Ty stops walking, and I have to turn around to look at him. He's gazing up at the clock tower that looms over this part of the campus. It's all brick, a nice, tall, imposing phallic symbol put there by men with high ideals and small minds, but I like it anyway. There's a bit of character in the molding, the splash of rust orange paint the original builders used around the clock face.

"That wasn't a line," Ty says as the wind grabs his dark hair with gentle fingers and brushes it over his forehead. He pulls the cigarette from his mouth and shifts his gaze to my face.

"Liar," I say as he moves forward and pauses next to me.

"Maybe," he tells me as bends over, hovers his lips above mine, close enough that I can feel his breath, but far enough away that he doesn't come close to touching the burning cherry of my cigarette.

"What do you want with me?" I ask him when he moves away and stretches his arms above his head. When he does that, the muscles in his arms slide beneath his skin just enough that it looks like the butterflies are moving their wings.

"Do I have to have an answer to that?" he asks me as he drops his arms to his sides. The courtyard has been quiet all this time, empty of everyone but Ty, myself, and a small flock of gulls that have drifted in from the bay, but now that classes are letting out, people are starting to brave the cold, crisscrossing the yard to get to the dorms and the other classrooms. They move between us while Ty waits for me to respond. "What do you want with me?" he asks finally when he realizes that I'm not going to say a damn thing. "You came to get me, so you must've had a plan in mind."

"I didn't," I tell him honestly. "I just wanted to see you. I missed you. I don't know why, but I did. You, on the other hand, are the one with the fucking plan. You took me to that stupid clinic for a reason and I'm guessing it's not because you wanted to get in my pants again. I don't know if I'll ever be able to have sex again after that nightmare." Ty smiles, but his dimples don't show, and shakes his head.

"What if I told you I had a plan, but that I didn't want to talk about it? Would that be okay?" I stare at him and try to figure out what to say. This relationship between Ty and me is taking more energy and effort than anything I have ever done before. Normally, this is something I would walk away from, give up entirely and forget, but I can't. Somehow, it's a little different this time.

"Fine."

"Now can I have your secret?" he asks with a sexy smirk that guys like him always use to get what they want. This time, at least, it isn't sex that he's after.

"Do we have time?" I ask sarcastically. "What about our sex addicts meeting?" People stare at me as they walk by, but I don't give a shit. Ty steps a bit closer, enough that students stop moving between us and have to go around, parting like the sea around a cluster of rocks.

"If I tell you something, you have to promise to forgive me."

"Maybe. What is it?" I blow smoke into Ty's face and he doesn't even blink.

"When you told me you had something to tell me, I panicked."

"Uh huh."

"I went out to a bar and I picked up a girl."

"That's fucking amazing, Ty," I tell him, feeling some of my stress leaking back. I toss my cigarette into a nearby garbage can and search for gum. I don't have any on me, so I go for another cigarette. Ty takes it between his fingers and puts it behind his ear.

"I had sex with her because I was afraid of you."

"How romantic. Why are you telling me this?" Ty takes me by the shoulders and looks into my eyes with his dark ones. When I get caught in them, I can't see much else. They're mesmerizing.

"I thought you were going to tell me that you loved me,

and I was afraid of that."

"I don't even know you," I tell him as I push his hands away. "Why would you think that?"

"Never," he says as I try to walk away. Ty grabs my hand and pulls me back. "I want you to scream with me."

"Scream?" I ask as I struggle to extract my grip from his, but he's strong and I end up giving in and letting him hold it.

"Yeah, scream with me. Yell, shout, let all your worries out."

"Here?" I ask, but I notice that the courtyard is getting quiet, leaving Ty and I alone with the clock tower once again.

"Why not?"

"What's the point, Ty? Are you trying to prove something to me? Why are you doing this?"

"Because I don't want to be afraid anymore."

How the hell do you say no to that?

"Fine, but we have to do it together. If you bail on me, I will ring your fucking neck." Ty grins and lets go of my hand. His silver bracelets bump against the rings on his fingers like a wind chime, filling the air with a merry tinkling.

"Ready?" he asks, but I'm not sure that I am. I nod anyway and take a big breath, pulling in the scent of winter and Marlboros and *change.* It's sitting heavy around me and although I didn't expect it, I'll roll with it because that's what I do. After all, I have nothing to lose anyway. Someone who struggles to find something to live for each morning and who despairs at night shouldn't be adverse to change. Otherwise they might end up like me.

"One," Ty begins as he tosses his cigarette into the trash. "Two." He smiles at me, nice and big. "Three."

Ty and I both take big, fat breaths, tilt our heads to the sky and scream. It's such a stupid thing to do that we both end up in fits of laughter, grabbing onto one another to stay standing as the students around us peek out windows and scratch their heads and wonder what the hell the two crazy people in the courtyard are doing.

Strangely enough, I'm proud to be one of them.

21

"My father was murdered."

These are the only words I get out before Ty realizes how big the scope of my secret is. He reaches out, wraps his arms around me and pulls me to his chest. I can barely breathe with my face crushed to the hard muscles of Ty's body, but it feels so damn good that I don't even bother to struggle.

"Are you up for getting something to eat?" he asks me

randomly. "Because I have a feeling this is something that shouldn't be rushed." Ty relaxes his grip on me just enough that he can pull his phone out of his pocket. "We have a few hours until the meeting, but … " He releases me and just stares, dark eyes searching my face for an answer. There's so much guilt in his, so much pain. He feels bad for sleeping with that girl, I can tell.

"But you're right," I tell him as I turn away and force him to follow me across a small bridge. We're deep in the campus' gardens now. It's getting close to winter so most of the bushes are bare and there are hardly any flowers, but it's still beautiful. There are evergreens towering above us, dipping into the cloudy sky and tasting the first drops of rain that are beginning to fall. Interspersed throughout are the bare skeletons of deciduous trees, naked of leaves but captivating nonetheless. They remind me of Ty in a strange way. "That's not it, not all of it." I pause and glance over at him. "It gets worse."

"Worse?" Ty asks with raised brows. "How much worse?"

"Tell me," I begin as the rain sprinkles Ty's dark hair and makes it glow beneath the lamps that are spaced out along the pathway. "Do you have a past?"

"We all have a past," Ty says as he reaches down and takes my hand in his. "But I can't talk about mine. Maybe someday but not now." I nod because I understand completely. "Come over to my place tonight," he blurts suddenly and I almost stumble. We were picking up our pace, heading for the covered walkways to get out of the rain, but now we're back to a crawl.

"Ty … " He holds up his hand and crosses his fingers together.

"No sex, no pressure, I promise. I want you to tell me your

story. All of it." I look at him skeptically, but he seems genuine, like he's telling me the truth. I want to believe him because as far as I know, he's only lied once. He said he didn't seek someone out to have sex with, but then he told me he picked a girl up in a bar. What am I supposed to do? "We'll have some beer and watch *The Walking Dead.*"

"I hate zombies," I tell him, and he smiles.

"Me, too," he says with a wink that makes his eyebrow ring sparkle. "Are we on then?" he asks as the rain turns from sprinkles to showers. I start walking backwards, expecting Ty to follow. He doesn't. I hold out a hand and his smile turns into a grin. "I'm not moving from this spot until you say yes." Ty's dark hair falls into his face and drips down his nose, taking him from handsome to godly. I never could resist a bad boy, especially not one whose shirt is plastered to perfect pecs, molded against a set of abs that would convince anyone to try whatever it was that he was selling. I can't stand seeing him in the cold rain with no coat and that sexy smirk on his face, so I sigh.

"Okay," I say as I shake my hand for emphasis. "As long as you get out of the fucking storm. Come on." Ty takes my hand and we finish our jog to safety. "I'm not religious, you know," I tell Ty as we slip into the one of the science buildings and head back the way we came.

"Neither am I," he says as we drip water across the red-orange floors. "What does that have to do with anything?"

"Sex Addicts Anonymous, they're a religious group." Ty stops walking for a moment.

"How do you know that?" he asks me with a cheeky smile. "You look 'em up before?" I shrug.

"We talked a little about them in one of my classes." Ty nods and we start to walk again.

"This group isn't actually a Sex Addicts Anonymous

faction, just a copycat." Ty points at my coat. "Second pocket down on your right." I snap open the button and pull out another brochure. The coat's kept I dry luckily, so even though it's wrinkled, I can still read it.

"The Sexual Obsession Group," I say and look up at Ty. "SOG?" Ty laughs and the sound echoes beautifully through the hallways. The brochure shows a girl and a boy painting a mural together with vibrant colors, laughing and smiling like they don't have a care in the world. Pure fantasy. I unfold the paper and scan the *Commitments* section.

While our group is not about abandoning the idea of sex, we do ask that members commit to a six month celibacy in order to get their thoughts, urges, and desires under control. Oftentimes, sexual addiction is just a cover-up for a deeper issue and if we can't reveal it, we may never find out what is really wrong.

I fold the brochure back up and stick it in the pocket. When I look up, Ty is watching me. I wonder about his past, but I won't ask again, not unless he gives me some indication that I should. He and I are so much the same that it makes me want to cry. I don't know why; it just does. Maybe it's because my past is rising to the surface like lava, getting ready to erupt and destroy everything around me? And if that's happening to me, then it's happening to Ty, too.

"I'm sorry about your dad," Ty says as he reaches down and wraps his big hand around mine. It fits nicely there, too nicely. It scares me just a bit, just enough that I let go and pretend that I need to fidget with my wet jacket.

"That's okay, I barely remember the prick," I say as I think about all the times he left home, left me and Beth and Jade and Zella alone with that woman, that *monster.* As I got older, I began to understand more and more about the man I have few memories about. My guess, and this is just a guess, is that it was hard for him when he found out that Jade wasn't his biological daughter. He'd known that my mother was a cheating whore, but I don't think he realized how far her treachery. How deep she'd already dug his grave. I hate that woman. "My therapist," I begin and realize that I haven't gone in weeks. Not since … I flick my eyes back up to Ty's. "My therapist thinks I have 'daddy' issues and that's why I sleep around, that I'm looking for a strong, masculine figure." Ty laughs.

"What a load of bullshit," he says. "I fucking hate therapists." I smile at him, but it's a weak smile, all tangled up with shadowy memories. I agree with him, though. The kind of boys I seek out are not at all the type of man that my father was. At least, I don't think so. I sigh, and it comes out sounding tired and broken. I don't like that at all. I shake my head to clear it. I wish I had picture perfect memories of my father, images of him smiling, the sound of his voice, the strength of his laugh, but I don't. I barely remember him at all as a person. Facts, facts I remember, but memories … I don't have many of those. "Why do you hate him?" Ty asks me, and I shake my head.

"We're getting too deep into my story," I tell him honestly. Once I start down this path, I won't be able to stop, I'm going to have to sit with the story of my life like a bad movie. I can only wonder, how is it going to end?

22

Ty and I are the first ones to arrive at the meeting.

The group leader is there, of course, but none of the other participants. My heart is in my throat, and I'm so tongue-tied that I let Ty introduce me.

"My name is Ty McCabe and this is my best friend, Never Ross," he tells the woman with skin like cocoa powder and eyes like emeralds. She's beautiful and powerful and so in control of herself that I'm mesmerized, by her and by Ty's words.

Best friend?

Have I ever had one of those? Do I want one? Best friend is really just a fancy word for someone that has their hand wrapped around your heart. *Best Friends Are the Soul Mates You Don't Sleep With.* Lacey has this plaque over her bed. I avoid looking at it because it's painted in pink on a cheery, white china backdrop. It hangs crookedly from a bit of twine. I always thought that in some strange way, it was put there by the universe to mock my pain. Yet here Ty is telling this woman with the steady hands, the confident smile, that I'm his. His best friend.

I look away from them both, unsure how to handle this situation. It's been a long time since I was so vested in something that I was actually afraid about how it would turn out.

The building around us is old and crumbly but pretty. Or it was once. Like many things, time has shredded it of its original beauty, covered up old details with layers of poorly applied paint, took what was once something grand, a mansion maybe or a boutique, and now here it is serving as a community center for this half of the city. I hear a basketball echoing from somewhere in the back of the building and smile.

And the downtrodden found refuge in dilapidation; and they were happy there because it was theirs and no one else's; bare of pretense and expectations, this place became a haven of solace and a sanctum for peace.

The poem that pops into my head is called *For Them The Wheel Turned* and it's by my favorite poet of all time, a one, Noah Scott. It suits this place so perfectly that I get this intense urge to chisel it into the wall of stone across from me. I don't think anyone would mind; there are already murals galore there, layered on top of one another, overlapping from the cement floor to the soaring heights of the ceiling. It's a massive wash of color that humbles at the same time it inspires. Impressive.

"My name is Vanessa Pickett," says the woman with the emerald eyes. She takes Ty's hand and shakes it firmly. When she sees me scoping out the wall of murals, she turns and looks at it, too, like she's seeing it for the first time, eyes darting along the stories pictured there. "It's pretty, isn't it?" she asks as I drop my gaze to her face. As if she can feel my eyes on her, she turns and looks straight at me. "What do you think of it, Miss Ross?" I shrug my shoulders and go for a cigarette. It's that or gum, anything that gives me an excuse not to talk, and I think I could use the nicotine right about now. Vanessa doesn't stop me. This room already smells like smoke anyway, and most of the windows are either broken or look rusted and seem to be stuck open.

"Would you like to help me set up the rug?" she asks, and I raise my brows.

"Rug?" Ty asks as he looks over at Vanessa. She laughs and gestures for us to follow her. There's a massive, metal box against the wall, wet on the top from the rain that's splattering in through the empty windows. Vanessa unlocks the padlock with a key and tosses Ty and I a pair of towels to dry off with. In the box is an assortment of things, once of which is a massive rug, rolled neatly and tied with a bit of rope. Ty wraps his towel around his shoulders and helps Vanessa lift it out and drag it across the floor to a dry spot in the center of the room. She unties the knot and kicks it out flat.

"I find that this works better than those horrible plastic chairs," she says, and I shiver. I couldn't agree more, so I help her pin down the curling edges with stacks of old books that she retrieves from her metal box. When we're done with that, she pulls out a plastic bag filled with yellow T-shirts. *Get SOGgy, they say. Sexual obsession* is *a disease. Find your cure today.* She gives one of these to Ty and one to me. "You don't have to wear them," she says with a white-toothed smile. "They're just for fun, but some people find it helpful to have a uniform of sorts. It makes them feel like they belong and we all need a little of that now and again, don't we?" Neither Ty nor I say a thing. He's as nervous as me, I can tell by the way he's pacing around. I, on the other hand, stand stone still, but my hands shake so badly that I tuck them in the pockets of the coat. "Have a seat if you'd like," Vanessa says as she sets a backpack down on the edge of the rug. From it, she removes a tablet along with a bag of colorful coins.

"Come on, Nev," Ty says, using the same nickname that Lacey gave me. I like it. A lot. I smile at him. "Put on the tee?" I raise my brows, watch as he lifts his shirt above his head and tosses it in a soggy heap on the floor. My pulse starts to race and my blood runs hot. Ty's midsection is a work of art, a collection of grooves and hard muscles that make up a wide chest and a thin waist that tapers down to perfect hips. His pants are hanging tantalizingly low, dragged down by the rainwater, and I catch a hint of deep grooves on either side of his body, that 'V' shape that a lot of women, including myself, go nuts for.

Shit.

I take my jacket off, suddenly hot, and put my cigarette into the glass ashtray that Vanessa sets out. I wonder what kind of woman I am that I'm horny just hours after a fairly humiliating STD test. *A crazy one,* is the only answer to that question, so I busy myself with slipping on the yellow tee over my tank top. Mine, at least, is dry thanks to Ty's coat. And the fact that he gave it to me doesn't escape my attention. I have heard Lacey say before that she only gives her jacket to girls she really likes because there's a chance she'll never get it back and she wants to be okay with that. Ty is okay with that? Or does he think that we'll be hanging out enough that he could easily retrieve it if needed? Either way, the thought is sort of terrifying. And nice. Both and neither. *God, how did I get into this mess?*

"Sit by me," Ty says as he settles himself on a corner of the rug and tugs me down next to him. Our knees touch and the air around me feels hot. There's a storm brewing outside, sending cold gusts of wind and water into the building and I'm *hot.* Wow. I really do need this meeting.

"So," Vanessa asks as she moves her finger across the screen of the silver tablet. She smiles and her eyes crinkle at the corners. "I know I spoke to you over the phone, Mr. McCabe, but do you have any questions about the process?"

"Uh, no, I'll just go with the flow," Ty replies, smiling without his dimples.

"How about you, Miss Ross?" I shrug and light another cigarette. Ty pulls it out of my mouth and sticks it in his with a wink. I get out another.

"I'm okay," I say, and Vanessa nods with a secretive, little smile that tells me I might not be. I let my eyes drift to the side and watch water drip down the wall and pool into a puddle on the floor. Moments later, they start to trickle in, a sea of people so ordinary that I wouldn't pick them out of a lineup. Ty and I are the strangest looking ones there. Especially Ty. Most definitely Ty. I notice that a few of the women notice him, let their eyes linger just a bit. To my relief, Ty doesn't look at any of them. In fact, he seems completely checked out. I touch his hand and he blinks like he's coming to. Then he leans over and whispers into my ear, sending chills down my spine.

"Whatever I say here, whatever I do, don't hold it against me." I nod and I know that I won't. How can I? Where's my high ground? That's right, I don't have any.

"Okay," Vanessa begins, lighting a series of small candles and sticking them in the center of the rug. "Now that we're all here ... " She lets her eyes trail around the twelve faces that are present, pausing for just a moment longer on mine and Ty's. "I'd like to introduce two new members to SOG. This fine gentleman here is Ty McCabe." Ty holds up a hand and gives a tight smile. I wonder if he wonders about getting up and leaving, just walking out. That's what I'm thinking about, even though I know I won't do it. The way I felt at the clinic, like I was right where I was supposed to be, that's how I feel here, too. "And the lovely, young woman next to him is Never Ross."

"Printed just like it sounds right across the top of my birth certificate," I say, use to getting stares and questions about my name. It is strange. Admittedly, I've never met another person with it. At least it makes it easy to tell me apart. The group claps and smiles, but I can see that they're looking at us like we're outsiders. This is not going to be easy.

"What we're going to do to start off the day is get to know Never and Ty, learn some of their secrets." Vanessa smiles, but I shift uncomfortably. I don't like sharing secrets, especially with myself. And there are a lot of them buried down inside, waiting for me to take notice, to take control. I swallow hard and look at Ty. He's staring right at me, through me maybe. God, we're the same, me and him. "Why don't we go around the circle, introduce ourselves, and say something that we feel represents the deepest part of us, anything at all. Is there anyone that would like to start?"

"I'll go first," Ty says, dark eyes still searching mine. It's making me nervous, so I look away. "My name is Tyson by birth," Ty says as he takes a drag on his cigarette. I'm just letting mine burn, watching the cherry crackle like fire. I don't want to inhale; I can't. I want to block out all of Ty's words, put him back in my dangerous boys category, forget about why he hurts and who he is, go home and cry. I want to do this because like Ty, I'm afraid, too. I'm terrified. I make myself sit still, prove to myself that I'm as brave as I'd like to believe I am. "But if you call me that, I won't answer. I lost my virginity at thirteen, got roped into the sex trade, and worked as a whore for a good portion of my adult life." I don't look at him. I won't look at him. I *can't* look at him. "I had male and female clients and I rarely used condoms. If I die tomorrow, it won't be a surprise." Ty's voice is so bitter that I have to squeeze my eyes shut to listen to him. *You brought us here,* I think at him frantically. *You opened up this Pandora's box.* I want nothing more than to slam it shut in that moment, let it fester and burn. What's so wrong with being tortured anyway? My emotions are on a roller coaster right now and it's making me sick. At least when I was unhappy, I was always unhappy. I can't stand these fluctuations; they sting too much.

"You sound pissed off, Ty," Vanessa says, and I look back at her. I won't look at anyone else, but I'll look at her. She's sitting up straight with her tablet in her lap and her green eyes locked on Ty's.

"Damn right I'm pissed off," he says, and I can see from the corner of my eye that he's running his hand through his dark hair. "I can't … I don't … " Ty tries to get me to look at him by putting a hand on my knee, but I push it off and let it fall to the rug. He's asking for my help. *Fuck.* When I went to find him today, I didn't expect this. I guess I expected some kind of fairytale crap, but this is the real world, the world where Ty and I got ourselves into trouble and are just now realizing that we need to get out. “I'm sorry,” Ty says as he takes a massive breath. “I've been preparing myself for this for the past few days. I had a speech planned, but I forgot all of it. Honestly, I'm a little freaked out.” Vanessa nods.

“Understandable,” she says. “Would you like to continue?” Presumably Ty shakes his head because Vanessa moves on, swinging her gaze to mine. My spine stiffens and I feel my fingers curling around my knees. I reach up suddenly and grab my cigarette, take a huge drag and try to hold the smoke in my lungs. “What about you, Never? Would you like to go next?” I blow out the smoke slowly, so very slowly.

“My name is Never, and I'm a sex addict. Can I go now?” There are some nervous chuckles around the group, but Vanessa sees right through me.

“That's great that you can admit that, Never, but we're not about twelve steps or confessions or any of that bullshit here. We're real people with real problems. Do you have a problem, Never?”

“I don't know,” I reply honestly. “Is being promiscuous a problem? Men have been praised for centuries for doing exactly what I'm doing. I go out, find guys I like, and fuck them. Maybe I'm just a stud?”

“Do you feel like a stud, Never?” Vanessa asks. She knows that I'm bullshitting her, and she doesn't like it. I *know* I have a problem. Looking for people to fill the holes inside of me is not going to make me better. They get in there and they break me up inside. They make me miss home and the possibilities that might've happened had I stayed. I dream sometimes that I never left that night, that I stayed with Noah Scott and got married. See, Noah Scott is the kind of guy you can take home to your family, show off, and know that at the end of the day, he'll be there for you. That's who Noah Scott was. See, this guy next to me, this Ty McCabe, he's one of the dangerous ones, the ones with pasts that burn like fire and melt everything around them.

"I don't know, Vanessa," I say feeling confrontational all of a sudden. "I stopped counting at forty." There's no reaction from the group, no murmuring, nothing. If they're judging me, they're doing it quietly.

"What do you love most about yourself?" Vanessa asks, and the most horrible thing about that question is that I don't have any answer. "Don't answer that yet," she says suddenly, like she's a fucking mind reader or something. "We'll come back to you. Ben, would you like to go next?" I finish my cigarette, toss it into the ashtray and start on another. And another. I start a new cigarette for every person who speaks, all ten of them, and when the circle finally returns to Vanessa, I feel sick. From the nicotine, from the smoke, from the stories, I don't know. I hear the words *empty, lonely, helpless, afraid.* They repeat these over and over again as they share bits of themselves with me. I smoke and stare out at them with tired eyes and a down turned mouth.

"My name is Vanessa Pickett, and I have worked as a professional escort, a stripper, and even a madam. I'm not proud of it, but I also can't claim I was forced into it or driven to it through abuse. I had a good life, and I was raised well, but there was something inside of me that sought out more. I was always seeking it, but could never find it." She's looking straight at me, waiting for some kind of reaction. I refuse to give her one.

"When my son passed away, I was forced to look at the world in a different way. I realized that I had missed out on his life. Spending time with people you love and who love you is the easiest path to recovering that part of yourself that's missing. Whether it's a lover or a friend or a child, the best place to find solace is in a warm heart."

"Or a warm bed," I say because I'm getting pissed off. I might've left my baggage at the clinic, but now I feel open and empty and bare. I don't like that. Not at all. My fear makes me angry, and right now, I want to rage.

"Tell me, Never," Vanessa says, trying to distract me with the bag of shiny coins that sits in front of her. "How many days has it been since you last had sex."

"A week." I don't look at Ty.

"And you, Mr. McCabe?" I hear him swallow.

"A week."

The group claps and Vanessa retrieves two, shiny, red chips from her bag. She passes them over to Ty who drops one in my palm. *Seven Days* is etched into the top. Great.

"This is the one thing we have adopted from the other addiction groups that are out there. It's a good reminder, something to keep in your pocket, a physical declaration of your commitment. We stop giving the chips out at six months. After that, if you're ready to have sex with someone, then that's your choice."

"Isn't it always my choice?" I snap, but Ty steps in before I can make an even bigger ass out of myself.

"Is it alright if Never and I act as each other's sponsors?" Vanessa nods and touches a finger to her tablet.

"Absolutely," she says as she glances at some of the other group members. "This isn't about rules or punishments or meetings, this is about saying what needs to be said, learning from others, and getting better."

"Thank you," Ty tells her honestly as I watch Vanessa pull out a blue chip. It says *One Month* on it, and all of a sudden, I am just so freaking pissed off that I can't sit still. I watch as some of the other group members celebrate milestones and feel this hot rage boiling inside of myself. I keep a lid on this, hold it back while people make dinner plans to celebrate being able to keep their dick in their pants, to keep their fucking legs closed. Good for them. Great for them.

"So, Ty, I'd like to ask you about your turning point. We all have them, something that changes our mind, that makes us aware of our problem. What's yours?"

I let my anger get the best of me once and for all and answer for him.

"He was afraid that I loved him, so he fucked somebody to forget about me."

"Never," Vanessa begins but I cut her off.

"Then he came over and fucked me. That's his turning point. Want to hear mine?"

"Come on, Never," Ty says, reaching out and trying to take my hand. I pull it away from him and rise to my feet. My breath is coming in short, sharp bursts, and I can't sit still. I look around the group, scan the faces that are raised to mine, and I don't see straight. I need to get out of here. Now.

"I have to go," I say, and then I turn and run away as fast as my legs can carry me.

23

Ty finds me a few hours later sitting on the swings outside his house.

I've been here all day, waiting for him, wanting to apologize. When I hear his footsteps and look up, he smiles at me.

"I went to your dorm, but you weren't there."

"Did you fuck anybody?" I ask, ready to get up and leave. I didn't. I wanted to, but I resisted the urge. I came here instead, ran all the way here and sat on this swing for three and a half hours waiting. For what, I don't know, but I did, and I want Ty to respect that.

"I didn't," he promises me.

"Liar."

"Never, if I had, I would tell you."

"You're the kind of guy that lies, that cheats, that – " Ty takes my chin in his hand and forces me to look at him. I try to jerk my gaze away, but he won't let me.

"Maybe. And you're the kind of girl that loves and leaves, that breaks hearts without even knowing that you're doing it. If you want, we could be good friends, Never."

"I've been nothing but honest with you," I tell him. "Can you do the same with me?"

"I'm willing to try," he says, and when I open my mouth to protest, he releases me and steps back. "That's the best I can do. I'm sorry you feel betrayed by me, Never, I really do, but I never intended for that to happen. Just tell me what you want from me, and I'll do my best to respect that."

"Ty, I have one chance left. If I give it to you, will you make sure that I don't regret it?"

"Of course," he says, but I don't think he gets it.

"I'm drowning in lies, McCabe. One more and I will sink. Do you understand me?" Ty and I stare at one another for a long time. After a few moments, I sit back down on the swing. Ty moves around behind me and wraps his hands around mine, curling our fingers around the chains.

"Okay, Never," Ty says. "Give me your chance, and I'll give you mine." I look up at him, crane my neck up so that I'm leaning back on the swing. When Ty starts to push me, I don't protest.

"So am I allowed back to come back to the group?" Ty

chuckles.

"Vanessa begged me to bring you next week. She says that you remind her of herself." I smile because that woman is strong, like a pillar. I'd like to be that way someday, too. "So no sex for six months?" I ask and Ty grins.

"No sex for six months."

"Should I get you tissues and lotion for Christmas?"

"Nah," Ty says. "I can't wait that long for it. I'll get them myself. What about you? Do you want a vibrator for Christmas?"

"I have three." Ty pauses and his dimples appear, deep and round in his perfect face.

"I knew it," he says and a chuckle escapes my throat. Ty pushes me harder and I rise into the sky, feet pointed towards the stars.

"Ty," I say because I think this is important. Whether Ty believes he did something wrong or not, I was angry with him, so I have to do this. "I forgive you." Ty stops the swing by wrapping his arms around my waist and pressing his face into my hair. I get chills down my spine and the mood at our dark, little playground goes from angry to happy to sad.

"Thank you, Never," he says and he sounds genuine. "I forgive you, too." I smile and tilt my face back. Ty presses a soft kiss to my lips. We don't linger and we don't use tongue, but there's intent there and a promise to try. At this point, what else can I ask for?

24

Ty takes me up to his apartment. It's the first time I've ever been, and I'm impressed. It's a one bedroom, one bath, with a good sized living room and a small, galley kitchen. Ty says the girl he picked up trashed it when he asked her to leave (not that I blame her), but it looks perfect to me.

There's a big, red couch with a pair of black pillows, a coffee table in the shape of an eight ball, and pictures on every wall, framed photos of vintage cars.

"My mom took those," Ty says, but he doesn't elaborate, and I don't ask, just follow him into his kitchen where he opens a stainless steel refrigerator and grabs a couple of beers. He opens mine for me and passes it over with a smile. I'm scoping out the kitchen now, touching bowls full of fruit and a stack of folded wash rags. Not bad for a young bachelor. "I know how to take care of myself," Ty says as he notices me looking. I point at an electric stand mixer and he grins. "I said take care of, not pamper," he tells me with a wink. "I won that at my work's Christmas party last year. If you want it, you can have it." I give him a look that says, *I don't know shit about cooking,* and take a swig of my beer. It's malty and smells like roasted caramel. I love it, but then, I'm not exactly a connoisseur of alcoholic beverages. I almost wish that I was, that I used alcohol instead of sex to make my problems go away. Seems like that would be less complicated than this.

Ty motions me to follow after him, past a small wooden table with a pair of chairs, and into the bedroom where his twin bed sits against the wall, rumpled and disheveled. There's a squat dresser against the wall opposite and a flat screen TV sitting on top of it. Ty has these big, black curtains over his windows that block out all the moonlight, but that I guess come in quite handy in the morning.

I want to ask Ty if he ever did business in here, if ever accepted money in exchange for false love, if this room is tainted. I keep my thoughts to myself, convinced that this is not the time or place for that. It doesn't matter anyway. What's done is done, and there's no taking it back. I push my trepidation and fear aside and look down at the bed.

"It's clean," Ty tells me as reaches down and straightens the comforter, the pillows. "I don't bring people into my bedroom." I raise my eyebrows and down half of my beer in one swig.

"What do you do with them?" Ty shrugs, but I don't press him for answers because I don't want to know. I decide that at the very least, I can sit in here without imagining Ty's cock sliding in and out of another woman. The thought makes me physically ill. *I am fucking jealous,* I realize which is ten shades of stupid because Ty and I are not a fucking couple. I don't want to be a fucking couple. I do not want a fucking boyfriend.

"Are you hungry?" he asks me. "There's a spicy curry stand that delivers from down the street, if you're into that kind of shit."

"I love that kind of shit," I tell him as he pulls out his phone. There's this weird moment in time where everything seems to slow as it drops down to the carpet in front of my feet. I bend down and pick it up out of habit, noticing too late that Ty is reaching out to stop me. The background on his phone is a photo of someone very, very familiar. "Ty?" I ask as I stare at hazel eyes flecked with green and ebony hair with one, angry, rebellious red streak. "I'm wearing the red dress I had on when we first met."

"I thought you were beautiful," he tells me with a smile. I hand him back the phone and he looks at the picture. I don't know when he managed to take it; I never saw him do it in those few, strange moments we shared in the bar. It's a nice picture, but it's a little weird. I shift uncomfortably. "I've taken a lot of pictures over the years."

"I don't care."

"Lots of women have graced this screen."

"Men, too?" I ask sarcastically. I didn't mean to. The little monster inside of me is still there, still making me do things I don't want to do. I apologize immediately, keeping my eyes on the poster that lines Ty's door. It's a pinup girl by Gil Elvgren. She's got a hammer in one hand and her thumb in her mouth, face twisted all innocent like, at odds with her sexy thigh highs and pointed bra. For just a split second, I wish I was as glamorous as her, and then it fades away and I'm happy to be a modern woman who can rock jeans and a T-shirt the day after she rocks a cocktail dress. I like having choices.

"I'm not gay," Ty tells me with a shrug. He sips his beer and grabs a cigarette out of a box on his dresser. It's not a Marlboro this time but a Djarum Black with cloves. They're banned in the US and I wonder where Ty got them from. I won't smoke them, but they smell good. Still, seeing that little, black cigarette in his mouth makes me want to quit. I don't know why; it just does.

"I never said that," I tell him, finishing my beer and standing up so that we're facing one another. "I'm sorry."

"Men pay better than woman, and it's easier to get clients."

"You don't have to explain yourself to me," I tell him as I turn around and walk into his kitchen like I own the place. I don't know how else to act. Ty and are not close, not really; we don't even really know each other yet I feel like I've *always* known him, like he's a part of me, my other half or something. I wonder, if he could read my mind, would he ask to me to leave like he did with the last girl? Would he stop coming around? Would I scare him away? It's only now that I'm even admitting these thoughts to myself. They're scary as fuck, and I don't know what to do with them. I don't know why I feel like this, and I don't like it. I wish I'd never met Ty McCabe.

I put my beer on the counter and open the fridge. Ty stops me with a hand on my arm.

"I don't have to explain myself, but I want to. I wish you were interested in hearing what I have to say."

"How do you know that I'm not?" Ty releases me and some of the anger goes out of his face. I make an effort not to slam the fridge and set the two beers on the counter before I turn to face him. He moves up next to me and pops both tops with a bottle opener he gets from inside a drawer. "You were saying something about curry?" I continue.

"Tell me about Noah Scott," he says as he dials a number on his phone. I sigh.

"To tell you about Noah, I have to tell you about everything."

"So do it," Ty says. "Tell me." He pauses. "Spicy curry or mild curry? Those are your only choices."

"No choice of meat?" I ask.

"I don't know what it is, and I don't want to know," Ty says as I hear a voice on the other end of the line. "It tastes good, and I'm not willing to risk never being able to eat it again."

"Spicy," I say and Ty grins.

"How did I know?" I tug on his nose ring, wondering how much it hurt, wondering why he thought it would be attractive to have a piercing in between his nostrils. It's quirky, I must admit, and it does suit the whole bad boy look he's got going on. "Two spicy curries," he tells the man on the other end of the line. "Yeah, yeah, this is Ty." Ty puts his hand over his mouth to block his voice from the receiver. "He's surprised because I only ever order one."

"You never ordered in for your girlfriends?" Ty hangs up without another word, and I think it's funny that he's on a first name basis with the curry stand.

"I never had girlfriends, Never," Ty says as he grabs my hand and pulls it away from his ring. He presses a kiss to my fingertips that only confuses me and pisses me off. I tug my arm back and cradle my fingers against my chest. "There were clients and there were fucks. There's not much more to it than that."

"I was in love once," I tell him. Ty's face falls.

"I've never been in love."

We stand in silence until the curry arrives at the door. If someone were to spy on us through the window, they might think we were nuts, but it works for us. It works for Ty McCabe and Never Ross and that's just the way things are.

25

"Start from the beginning," Ty says with a Marlboro hanging out of the corner of his mouth and a box of takeout in his hands. I'm sitting across from him at this tiny, little bistro set that's so rusty I can't even tell what it might've looked like before. Ty says it came with the apartment and that it was this way when he moved in. He says it was the only thing he didn't throw away when he cleaned. "I mean the beginning-

beginning. Start when you were born."

"You really want to go back that far?" I ask with a sigh. Ty is right. This curry is *amazing.* It tastes like a hundred countries and a thousand plants and deserts and bazaars and all sorts of other strange, wonderful things. He's also right about the meat. I don't know what it is, and I don't want to know. It better not be cat. I take a sip of my beer and grab the cigarette from Ty's mouth. "Fine, but first, I want to know what your chance is. This is my last one, so if I'm going to trade it for yours, I want to know what I'm getting."

"You're getting a fucked up mess," Ty says as he twirls his plastic fork around in his food.

"Good, then it's an even trade." Ty smiles and we both turn our heads as a couple police cars flash past, brightening up the darkness on this side of the city for just a moment before they disappear. From here, Ty and I have a view of all the disturbing nightlife that calls this place home. I see hookers on the corner and drug dealers in the alleys, but above it all, I see the city stretching away, rising and falling, old buildings mixing with new. It's pretty if you tilt your head to the side and squint. It's all about perspective. "But what's it about? How do I know I can trust you with mine?"

"I meant to tell you, before, about the phone, that I've never left a picture on it that long."

"You're changing the subject," I tell him as I lean back and let the cool breeze tease along my skin. Soon, it's going to be unbearably cold out here, but for now, it's just right.

"Even after you called me a whore, I left it up. I've left it up this whole time."

"Why?"

"I don't know."

More silence.

"I was born approximately twenty-one years ago in a

dingy, little hospital in some Midwest dump." Ty grins and steals the cigarette back from me. "My mother was young, eighteen I think. She had my sister, Beth, when she was sixteen." I raise my hand up for him to see and he presses his palm against it, rings and all. My heart flutters strangely and for a moment, I can't breath. I curl my fingers around his and manually open my chest for air. It isn't easy. I point to my thumb first and then to each subsequent finger. "Beth, me, Jade, Zella, India." I pause and hold up my other hand. Ty takes this, too. I don't know why he keeps touching me like this, but I might have to ask him to stop. It's too confusing, too … I don't even know. Just too. Too. Too. Too. "Lettie, Lorri," I finish as I squeeze his hand with mine. When I'm finished, we both pull away at the same moment and focus our eyes on the parking lot. There's a couple with a baby down there, trying to figure out how to get a car seat into the back of their dinky, little sedan.

"Seven girls, five fathers." Ty doesn't judge me which is nice. He just sits there and listens, sipping his beer and smoking his cigarette. I love the way the wind plays with his hair, teases his face with it and curls it gently with its fingers. It's poetic somehow. "My mom got married to my dad when she was pregnant with Beth. Then they had me and then Jade and then Zella." I sigh. "But my mom cheated. A lot. Constantly." I hold out my hands, and I notice that they're shaking again. I grab my beer and hold it so that I have something to do with at least one of them. That way, maybe Ty won't notice. "I think my therapist was dead wrong about everything," I tell Ty with a small smile. "Maybe because I didn't tell her the whole story?"

"Or maybe therapists just suck?" Ty adds. I laugh, but it sounds hollow and empty. Recanting this story is not the easiest thing for me, but it's part of the process, part of this whole healing binge that Ty has just started me on, this path through thorns and rocks and swamps, this path that isn't easy but that has to be traveled. If not, I doubt I'll make it long enough to get my degree.

"I have 'mommy' issues, Ty. If there's anything that's wrong with me, that's it." I close my eyes and try to remember what it was like to be at home, with Mom hating Dad and Dad despising Mom and all of us in the middle of something we didn't understand. My mind paints me a nice picture, depicts the events and the scenes and the faces the way they should be, but I know it's not real. I don't *really* remember the way it all went down. "Jade was not my father's daughter, not biologically, but he loved her anyway." I pause and a bit of something comes into my head. *Custody.* Was that what it all boiled down to? Is that why my father died? I swallow hard and Ty can tell that's something's wrong.

"Are you okay, Never."

Tears prick my eyes.

"I can't do this," I say and Ty leans over, puts his hand on my knee and just waits. That's the one plus side of hanging out with other tortured souls. They know when to press, when to stay quiet, and when to stop. Usually.

"You can," Ty whispers, but I've kept my past locked away for so long that opening it up has opened me up. It's burst out before I was completely ready and torn me to shreds. I drop my beer to the pavement of the patio where it crashes into a million pieces, just like me. I'm breaking, cracking, splitting. I had thought, at first, that Ty's voice could slither into my psyche and rip me apart, but now that he's sitting there across from me and speaking so softly that I can barely hear him, I know that that isn't true, not entirely. He has that ability, sure. He has it because I'm attracted to him, like there's this magnetic force between us pulling us together and pushing us apart. He has it because I'm so sure that he could break me if he wanted to. That's the part I was right about. What I was wrong about was Rick. Rick could not have glued me together like I'd imagined. He couldn't have because his pull wasn't strong enough, not like Ty's. Ty's. Ty McCabe's.

I gasp like I'm coming up for air, and suddenly, I'm just sitting there with these big, fat tears rolling down my face. I think my nose is running, too, and I'm hiccuping, finding it hard to stop my hands from shaking so bad that they hurt.

"Never," Ty says as he pulls me off my chair and onto his lap. He wraps his arms around me and holds me while I cry. And cry. And cry.

I cry into Ty's perfect shoulder and breathe in the scent of tobacco on his shirt. I run my fingers through his soft, soft hair, and I wait for the feelings to subside, to die down, to relax into me instead of take over me. At first it doesn't seem as if they're going to. Normally, in this situation, I would look for someone to have sex with, but I know I can't do that anymore. If I want to deal with my past instead of just bury it, I have to let shit sit with me for awhile.

"Tell me about Noah," Ty says and I laugh through my tears. "That's better," he says as I sit back and he runs his thumb under my swollen eyelids. "That's the sound I want to hear."

"Scoping out the competition?"

"There is no competition," Ty says and the words, I think, are fiercer than he meant them to be. *What the hell?* Ty smiles and moves on as if he hadn't said that. "So. Noah Scott. Was he bigger than me?"

"Ty," I say, but it's funny enough that I laugh a little bit, that I pull back from my fears enough that I can breathe, that I can speak without hiccuping. "I don't remember," I tell him honestly. "What I do remember is that the first boy I ever loved had blue eyes and blonde hair. He had a perfect smile and a soft touch. He's studying business now," I add as an afterthought. I can look at Noah online, spy at him though rose colored glasses, see what he wants me to see, but I can't really know what's going on with him, if he missed me after I left, how he felt when he woke up alone and found my note. "We started dating freshman year of high school," I tell Ty, wondering vaguely what he was like in school. If we'd found each other then, would we have suffered like this? Did we need all of this pain and hurt to make us who we are or would we have fallen together like a fairytale couple, gotten married, had kids? "We dated up until I left. He used to write me poems." Ty smiles.

"Is that why you hated it when I tried to quote you poetry?"

"Noah always had his own words. I guess I can't stop comparing everyone I meet to him."

"Why not just call him?" Ty asks as if the solution is that simple, as if I can just pick a phone and call a boy I haven't seen in five years.

"That didn't go over so well with Beth," I say. I have over a hundred missed calls on my phone now. I looked when I was in the bathroom earlier. I've thrown my sister a line, and it's only a matter of time until she finds me. "My last name isn't Ross by the way." I pause. "Well, it is now, legally. I was born Never Regali."

"Ah," Ty says, still wrapped around me, chin resting on my shoulder. This is a rare thing for me, snuggling a guy like this. I tell this to Ty.

"I haven't had anyone hold me since Noah."

"Was he your first?" Ty asks and, determined to tell him the truth, I answer honestly.

"Yes."

"Why did you leave?" Ty asks, digging straight down through all the bullshit to the root of the problem, to the core of my issues and my pain, to the seed that started it all.

"You saw the video," I tell Ty. "You heard her announce her engagement?" He nods. "Well," I say as I wait for Ty to light a cigarette. It's a Djarum Black this time, and without hesitation, I pluck it from his fingers. Smoke kills, but secrets kill faster, and if I'm going to say this aloud, for the third time in my life, I'm going to need it. "The man she was planning on marrying was the one who killed my father."

26

Ty doesn't ask me to explain anymore after that, but I do anyway. I tell him how my father was murdered, how he was strangled from behind for eight long minutes. Six minutes where I sat and did nothing, just watched as the man that loved me, that I loved back, died with his eyes glassy and his face purple, choking on vomit and bile. I've blocked a lot of it out, fortunately, or I might not just be a sex addict. I might be a whole lot worse. I've forgotten the gurgling sounds that he made as he died, and the way his body slumped to the floor. I forgot the long hours where I sat there, still as a statue with my arms wrapped around my knees.

What I didn't forget was my mother's face when I told her what happened, when she walked in with Beth and Jade and Zella and found me sitting there. I remember how dry her face was, how she didn't cry at Dad's funeral, how she called me a liar.

"He was Jade's biological father, you know," I tell Ty whose eyes are focused on the floor but whose ears are all mine. "He disappeared for awhile after that, but when he came back into town, my mom started dating him again behind my back. All my sisters knew when she got engaged; she told them all, but she didn't tell me, Ty."

"So you found out at the performance?"

"I confronted her," I continue. I bet my eyes are glassy now, glazed over with old memories. Now that I've started them, they won't stop. If Ty taped my mouth and chained me up, my brain would run through them again and again, never stopping until someone was there to hear. Someone has to hear, and I couldn't be happier that that person is Ty McCabe. "I told her again what I'd told her before, that he'd killed my dad." I shake my head here because this is the hardest part to tell, the part where my sisters gang up on me, where they belittle me and side with my mother. This is the part where Beth slaps me, *hard*, cracks me right across the face because she doesn't want to hear me say anymore. This is the part where a piece of me dies, where I know they all care far more about themselves then they do about me. "They didn't believe me. Jade, especially, was angry."

Her eyes flash from hazel to black, filled with a rage that I, alone, can't possibly be responsible for. No single person could be responsible for that much hate, but it can be targeted at one person and that person is me.

"I hate you, Never," she hisses at me. "From the bottom of my heart, I hate every last inch of you."

I blink a couple of times to regain focus and grab Ty by the chin. His dark eyes are sympathetic, understanding. One day, he'll give me his story. I just have to be willing to wait for it.

"They said their worst, did their worst, and I ran out on them. I went to Noah knowing that it was the last I'd ever see of him. I gave him the best performance I could give, danced for him in a way I could never have danced for anyone else. We slept together and I snuck out before dawn. I left and I never went back."

"Wow," Ty says, and he tries to smile to lighten things up. "That's quite a story."

"Isn't it?" I ask as I inhale and watch a pair of teenage boys start a fight on the street corner. Now that it's out there, now that I've said it, made into words the thoughts that have been swimming in my head all this time, I feel healed, just a little. This is only the beginning, I know that now, but it's a good beginning, a start to something beautiful. "Winter break's coming up, Ty. I think I should go out there. I think I have to see them."

"I think that you're right," he tells me as I stand and stretch. Ty runs his hands down my sides and pauses when he catches me looking at him. "The more I learn about you, the more I want to know." I don't know how to respond to that; I'm not prepared for it. I smile at Ty and grab his hands, pull him to his feet, and put my forehead in the crook of his neck.

"You promised me zombies," I tell him as he lifts my head up and grins.

"I did, didn't I?" Ty asks and I can tell he feels what I'm

feeling, like there's this invisible string wrapped around the two of us that wasn't there before.

"Show me," I say and he does. We sit together on his couch and we drink and we eat and we walk, and I know that we care about each other because we *don't* have sex. Later, I fall asleep and wake up to Ty carrying me. He puts me in his bed, lays me down gentle, and steps back. He doesn't try to touch me or sleep me with, and he certainly doesn't kick me out. *I'm the first girl in his bed,* I think as I curl into a ball and wrap the blankets around my shoulders. As strange as it sounds, it's comforting and my heart lulls me to sleep with a gentle, peaceful lullaby.

I wake up early the next day, look at the clock and get dressed for class, putting on my yellow SOG tee and not caring what anyone thinks about it. When I head into the living room, I see Ty lying shirtless on his back on the couch, chest rising and falling with every breath. I move over to him and stare down at his face. His sexy lips are curved in a meaningless frown, and his eyelids are fluttering like butterflies. I brush Ty's hair from his forehead, plant a kiss on his cheek, and disappear out the front door. In his sleep, he smiles.

27

When our next SOG meeting rolls around, Ty and I head there early to help Vanessa set up the rug. When she sees me, she smiles and acts like nothing unusual happened last week. I don't apologize for storming out because I don't believe that I owe anyone an apology. I did what I had to do in that moment, and I'm proud of myself for it. I was hurting, yes, and maybe I overreacted, but I can still feel, so there's hope for me. The ones that have forgotten how to feel, those are the ones that are lost. I'm still here, and Ty can save me if I let him. Just as I can save him if he lets me. We're not there yet, but we're now two weeks celibate and the recipients of a pair of orange chips. I've turned my red one into an earring and I plan to do the same with this one.

"Never," Vanessa says as the meeting begins, as the other members sit down and smile at me, nod, raise a hand in acknowledgment of my presence. A girl with bleach blonde hair and bright eyes leans over and tells me that, *You're not the only one.* I smile back at her and hope that whatever it is that Vanessa is going to ask, I can answer. "Have you thought about the question I posed last week?" I stare back at her and for the life of me, I can't remember. She chuckles softly and sets her tablet down on the rug. "I asked you what it was that you loved most about yourself."

Ah. That.

I nod and reach inside my coat for gum, pausing when I realize what I'm doing. I'm trying to weasel my way out of answering the question again. I still don't have an answer for her and most importantly, I don't have one for myself.

"Can I tell you what I love most about Never?" Ty asks as I turn in slow motion to look at him. Love? He loves something about me? Is that the same as loving me? I swallow and avoid that train of thought. It might lead to a wreck of gnarled metal with my heart in the center of it. I don't think I could handle that.

"Can I tell you what I love most about Ty?" I say, and I don't notice it then, but everyone around me is smiling big and goofy, recognizing something between us that even we don't see yet. Ty McCabe and I are falling in love.

"Of course," Vanessa says, emerald eyes sparkling. "Please do."

"I think you have an incredible capacity to love," Ty says and then because he's been too serious, he has to go and make an ass out of himself by grinning and saying, "And a tight ass." I roll my eyes as chuckles wind their way through the group, but inside, I'm grinning, too. There might still be darkness around me, but when I'm with Ty, I'm standing in a spotlight.

"What I love most about you," I say and toss one out there for the group to grin at. "Is your rhythm." I snap my fingers and I see that some of the ladies are smiling. The guys don't get it, at least none of these ones do. "It's not about the size of the hammer," I say. "It's the pace at which you swing it." Ty laughs, and I'm happy to see his face bright. His dimples are round and perfect, proving that the reaction I'm getting is as real as any I've seen before. "But truthfully," I say. "The best part about you is your soul. It's a piece of tortured beauty."

"Thank you Never," he tells me and even if nobody else understands what I mean, Ty gets it.

28

"Grr," Lacey says as she leans back on her bed and drops into Trini's lap. "I can't fucking figure out this formula." Trini touches her forehead affectionately, but doesn't say a word. She keeps her nose buried in her chem book and sighs. I don't respond either. Midterms are coming up fast and suddenly, time seems like this rare but precious thing, something that slips away in the blink of an eye. It's kind of sad because I've been spending these lazy afternoons with Ty, just lying around on his bed and talking or swimming in the pool at his apartment building, just random stuff like that. Telling him my secret has improved my life drastically. I feel like we're both sharing the weight of it now, and it makes it easier for me to go to bed at night and get up in the morning. In fact, I haven't cried *once* since my first night sleeping at Ty's house. I'm over there a lot now which is kind of nice actually.

I'm looking at a printout of paintings, trying to memorize artists' names and dates. It's better than 'interpreting' the work, trying to find a meaning for every little detail, but it's still unbelievably boring. When the door swings open and Ty walks in, I barely notice, determined to keep my nose to the grindstone.

"Never," he says and something about his voice scares the shit out of me. I look up and see that he's sweating, just soaked. His white T-shirt is see-through now, and I can actually make out the spots where his nipples are hiding beneath the fabric. It would be sexy if it wasn't so terrifying. This is the first time I have ever seen him without his piercings in. He just has these little holes in the spots where they're supposed to go: on the left side of his lip, his nose, his right eyebrow.

"What's wrong?" I ask as I set my study guide aside and touch the back of my hand to his forehead. He doesn't feel hot, just normal, like there's no way he could be sick. His eyes look okay, too, dark but not feverish, and his skin is a bit washed out but not flushed. Ty hands me a pair of envelopes from SHS.

It takes me a second to realize exactly what it is that I'm holding.

The results. The test results. The future direction of both our lives depends on what's inside these white envelopes, what's printed on this paper.

"Hey Ty," Lacey says, but he doesn't even look at her. He can't look at her because he's too busy looking at me. I stand up and my computer chair goes flying, topples over and crashes to the floor as I take both envelopes in my fingers and seriously debate burning them right then and there. If I burn them. I won't ever have to know. If I do, I can't move on. It's a tough decision but one with only one obvious answer.

"I have to go," I tell Lacey and she starts to protest.

"You told me not to let you so much as sleep, eat or piss during the next few days, Never. Where do you need to go?" I turn towards her and I bet I look like Ty now, sweaty and disheveled and all around weird. It's easy to look like that when you're holding your life's judgment in your hands. Every mistake I have ever made is going to be tested, weighed; any punishment that could be exacted on me will be doled out now. I could get through this clean, move on with my life and survive, or I could find out that I'm destined to die. The odds are not good.

"I have to go and learn my fate," I tell Lacey and who the hell could argue with that? Ty and I grasp hands, but I remain in control of the test results as we walk through the hallways of the dorms and pause in the elevator. Normally, we both like to take the stairs. Today, it's just far too much effort. My mind is too busy contemplating *what-ifs* and *what-nows.*

"If I have something … "

"Then we both probably have it," I tell him, trying to smile though this isn't exactly something that I should be smiling about.

"If I have something," Ty repeats again. "Will you stay with me?"

"Of course," I respond without hesitation. "You're my best

friend." I wink at him as we climb off the elevator and march through the lobby of the building, like we're promenading death, swinging it in circles in a crowded ballroom. Neither of us is seeing straight or moving lithely, it just isn't possible with all of this stress bearing down on us, threatening to crush us beneath its weight. Some people might have torn open the envelopes right away, taken the suspense away, but that only works if the results are good, and Ty and I are pretty much positive that ours are bad. If we drag this out, even tough it hurts, it might help keep us sane in the long run. These last, few moments of not knowing are better than adding more moments of fear or pain or despair. "Where do you want to do this?" I ask him at least as we pass out the glass doors and into the cold, gray of the November fog. It rolls off the bay and hangs salty in the air, not exactly the most pleasant of weather. I wish for sunshine with a fierceness that could kill.

"My place," Ty says and he takes my hand and walks me the few miles to his house in silence. When we get there, Ty hands me one of those Djarum Blacks that I said I would never smoke and a cold beer from the fridge. I take both without a word and sit down at his table, the two white rectangles fanned out in front of me.

"Should we each open our own?" I ask because I'm not sure how to go about doing this. I also know that I am never, ever going to go through this again. I've put myself through hell and back and now I'm paying for it. All those times I retreated to back rooms at party, laid on my back for a guy whose face is now a blur, spread my legs for a nameless shadow of a memory, I was hurting myself ten times worse than the memories could ever do. Ty is the same way, so he knows. I can look him right in the eye and think these things and see it all reflected back at me.

"Sure," Ty says because he doesn't know what to do either,

and we're both nervous for one another, both hardly able to breathe. "But you have to tell me right away."

"Ditto," I tell him as we both shred the paper with shaking fingers, pull out folded pages that mean everything and nothing all at once. Ty's eyes fly down his page, take it all in before I can even unfold mine. When he gets to the end, he rolls his gaze back to the top and starts over.

"I'm clear," he tells me as he hands me the page. "Never, I'm clear." I look down the list, at all the places where it says *negative* and am more grateful in that moment than I've been in any other in my life. No matter what happen to me now, Ty will live. Ty will be okay. This slows me down on my own results because in light of Ty's, they don't seem so important. Somehow, that asshole has made me care so much about him that I practically sob with relief. Or I will, as soon as I know my own fate.

I unfold my own letter, but before I can read any of the words, I close my eyes in cowardice, pinch them shut tight and sit there in absolute silence.

"What is it, Nev?" Ty asks, and I can hear in his voice that he's desperate to know, maybe even more desperate than I am. He wants me to be safe, wants me to live. I can see that getting his results back did nothing to assuage his fears. They were all for me, always for me. I take a deep breath, force my eyes open and my gaze down and read the words. *HIV – negative. Chlamydia – negative. Gonorrhea – negative. Herpes – negative. Pregnancy test – not pregnant.*

I have just dodged the proverbial fucking bullet.

When I look up at Ty, I have tears in my eyes. He mistakes this for sadness and collapses to his knees. Right then and there he falls for me in more ways than one. Ty McCabe makes a whole lot of decisions regarding Never Ross in that moment that I don't know, that I'm not privy to for some time to come.

"What is it?" he whispers and what he really means is, *What's going to kill you?* I reach out, cup his face with my hand and tell him the truth in all its beauteous, righteous glory.

"I'm going to live."

29

“Holy fucking shit!” I shout as I leave the lecture hall and find Ty waiting for me in the courtyard. He picks me up as soon as I walk over to him, swinging me in a circle, warming me with a welcoming hug that I know Lacey is jealous of, even if she doesn't admit it. Trini must still be in class and is nowhere to be seen. When Ty sets me down, I see that he's grinning. He looks awfully cute in his winter coat. It's puffy and has fur around the collar, giving him this look that guys only ever have in romance movies. "I did it," I say as I put my hands on my hips and watch my breath hang in the cold air. "I finished out the semester without killing anybody." *Or fucking anyone.*

"Congratulations," Lacey says as she gives a tight-lipped smile to some boys who are checking her out. She's wearing a T-shirt that says *Lipstick Lesbian* on the front. I don't think she could be anymore obvious about it, but poor Lacey is hot. She's that perfect blond goddess with the golden legs and the big, blue eyes. I guess we all have our crosses to bear. "What are you going to do for break?" she asks, and I shrug because I haven't the slightest clue. I've been toying with the idea of going home for awhile, but I don't know how to make that decision. Do I call? Do I just show up? What if they turn me down, tell me to go away? Even worse, what if they beg me to stay? What do I do with Ty? "Trini and I are going to spend some time at my uncle's cabin," Lacey says dreamily. Ty and I exchange a glance and a smile. When my phone beeps, I glance at it absently, expecting another missed call from Beth but instead find that I have a text message. The only people that would be texting me are standing on either side of me, cheeks and noses pink in the frigid air. Beth hasn't messaged me yet, but I check anyway, just in case it's her.

I don't recognize the number it came from, but I do recognize the area code. This is a message from home. I open the text and read it, convinced that the universe is playing tricks on me, fucking with my mind, my insanity.

The text message is from Noah Scott.

I drop the phone to the pavement and don't bother to stop Ty when he bends down to pick it up.

Your sister gave me your number. I miss you, Never. I'd love to see you. Give me a call.

At first, I'm crying because I don't know what to say or do or think. I dash the tears away quickly before Lacey gets a chance to see them, but Ty saw. I know he saw.

I swallow my emotions and look up at Ty. He has a detached sort of look on his face, like he can't quite believe it himself. Lacey remains oblivious, more concerned with Trini and why she isn't here yet.

"I hope she's doing okay on her exam. This is the one that she's most worried about." Ty and I ignore her and exchange a heated sort of a look. His dark eyes are flickering like a dying fire, and I'm sure mine aren't much better. I think a lot about Noah, and I tell Ty every single time I do. I've told him that I thought Noah might've been my fairytale ending. I've told him that the sex I had with Noah was the most meaningful I've ever experienced. I tell Ty a lot of things. What he probably thinks but that he doesn't tell me is that there's a definite possibility that I'm turning Noah into some kind of unattainable goal, making him this perfectly godly standard that no man can match up to. I'm willing to deal with that, but I need Ty to help me realize that; I need him to step in and convince me otherwise.

"What do I do?" I ask him, and notice that his eyes are a little glassy, too, a little dewy. What is he thinking? What's going through his mind right now? Things have been good between us, great actually.

"I don't know," he tells me honestly. "That's up to you to decide." I look down at the phone as he hands it to me, at the single text message from my past and I'm suddenly unsure. I've been making a lot of progress lately, but I don't know what to do about this. "Can I make a suggestion?" Ty asks as he leans down, grabs my hands and pulls me to him. Without another word, he leans down and kisses me. Heat sears straight through me, takes hold of my trembling body and burns. That addiction that Ty is for me, that wrongness and that pain, it's there now and it's pulsing, making my lips hurt, my heart seize up, my eyelids flutter. And Ty knows it. Fuck him, but he knows exactly what he's doing.

"Aw," Lacey says from behind us. I push back from Ty enough that I can take a breath, that I can look into his face and try to figure out what it is that he's feeling. Jealous? Scared? It's hard to say. I think he's shutting down and that scares me even worse. "You guys are so cute together," she says as she presses a kiss to both our cheeks. "But I see Trini down the hill. I'm going to go meet her. See you after break?" I nod absently because I'm too concerned with this sudden development in my life. I am walking a tightrope here, any bit of wind is liable to knock me over. "Call me!" Lacey shouts as he disappears and leaves Ty and me alone with the dead tree and the little brick wall.

"Want to come over?" Ty asks me, and I know for certain that this time, it's a loaded question. Old habits die hard. It's too true. I nod my head and let Ty take my hand. If he wants to convince me to stay, then I'll stay, I'll do whatever he wants me to do because I'm in love.

30

Ty's hot mouth is on my neck, and I find myself taking short, sharp, little breaths as I press my shaking hands to his chest. If I sleep with him again, I'll be making the biggest mistake of my life. He's the first real friend I've ever had, and I don't want to cheapen the feelings that are simmering between us. We made that mistake once before, and we survived. We've been through a lot since then, and I know that if I lose him now, I will never be whole again. Ty is my other half, lover or no, and just being around him is enough for me.

"Ty," I say, trying my best to sound stern. Instead, my voice comes out like a butterfly, flutters against Ty's hair and swirls it gently against my lips. I moan and find that my fingers are now curled in the fabric of his T-shirt.

"Never," he says back to me, the word like fire against my skin. In those two syllables, I hear how he feels about me. He thinks he's in love. Ty McCabe thinks he's in love with me. He doesn't say it aloud, but I can tell. Sex isn't the best way for me to show my feelings; I've abused it for far too long that it has somehow lost some of its meaning. I try to tell Ty this, but I can't speak with his lips on my throat and his hand sliding across the nape of my neck.

I run my own hands down his chest and put them beneath his shirt, on the hard plane of his belly. His muscles contract as I press my fingers into them, touching, feeling, absorbing the man, the complication, that is Ty McCabe. All the while, my mind is racing in circles trying to talk me out of this.

"Kiss me," Ty says and it's not a question, it's a request, albeit a gentle one. His voice is softer than I've ever heard it. His words are naked, stripped of all the bullshit that's happened to him, all of the horrible things that mirror my own life. Ty and I are like twins, like two halves of the same whole. They say that opposites attract, but Ty and I are very much the same and the attraction between us burns brighter than the sun. "Kiss me," he says again and I do.

Our lips touch and the darkness that's always made up my life, parts like a curtain, opens up wide and flashes me the sun. Ty's kiss, his touch, his words, our friendship, all of it runs over and through me, and suddenly, I'm pulling away because I can't breathe.

"Ty," I say as he follows after me, and I sit down hard on

the edge of his bed. "You mean more to me than sex." It's kind of a weird thing to say, but I know he gets it, and I hope he feels the same way.

"I know that," he tells me as he puts his hands on his hips and tries to breathe.

"So let's not do this," I say as I fall back into the messy covers and try not to think about how many girls Ty might've fucked in this apartment. "I like things the way they are. You're my best friend, my reason for getting up in the morning, the only thing in this world that convinces me that it's worth the effort to breathe." He sits down next to me and sprawls out on his side like he's done a million times in the blur of afternoons we've spent together. When Ty brushes the hair from my forehead, the feel of his fingertips against my skin is like torture. He doesn't mention Noah. Neither of us mentions Noah.

"Why do you say things like that?" he asks with a smile. "It makes it hard for me to one-up you." I roll my eyes and try not to think about how tender my lips feel.

"At this point, *not* having sex with you is about the best way for me to show that I care. Besides," I reach into my pocket and pull out my celibacy chip. It's bright blue and shimmers like a gem in the small shaft of sunlight that's managed to penetrate Ty's heavy, black curtains. *One Month.* "You don't really want to miss out on next month's, do you? I hear that it's purple."

"Never … "

"And anyway, I stopped taking the pill after that first meeting, and I don't have any condoms around. I never used them anyway." I stop talking and almost choke on the feelings that sweep through me. I dodged so many bullets that it's not even funny. For Ty and I both to be free of any STDs is a miracle that defies the statistics of our current world. Ty knows me too well now. He knows that I'm babbling because I don't have anything real to say. "You're supposed to be my sponsor, you know. This is like asking an alcoholic to come to a bar with you."

"You're not a fucking alcoholic," Ty says as he pulls the celibacy chip from my fingers. "Let's use a different comparison. What if you were a food addict? You can't just stop eating. You just have to stop eating *everything,* right?" I try to reach for the chip, but Ty throws it across the room where it hits the wall and falls to his dresser. "And fuck purple, Never, I want you."

"Ty," I say, but I don't know what else should come after that word, so I just stop talking. I try to turn away from him, but he grabs my hips and pulls me back.

"You can't run from this forever," he says as he leans down and presses a series of warm kisses to my neck, working his way down to my collarbone. I grab him by the hair and pull his face up to mine.

"Taking me to that meeting was your idea, and now you're pissed because I'm actually following the rules? I thought you wanted me to stop having sex. I thought *you* wanted to stop having sex." Ty laughs and scoots forward, so that his hip is partially atop mine.

"Wrong," he tells me as he gives me a dimpled smile. "My goal was for us to stop having sex with people we didn't know, didn't like, didn't care about. My goal was to stop you from having sex with other guys."

"Why?" I ask defiantly, reaching up and putting a hand between Ty and myself. My fingers splay open against his chest. Ty smiles and uses one arm to prop himself up and the other to brush the hair from my forehead.

"Because you're mine," he says and then he leans down,

forcing my arm out from between us and around his neck. I'm weak when it comes to Ty McCabe. I don't know when it happened or why but somehow I've been roped into falling for one of these dark boys with the angry pasts, one of these boys that I've always fucked but never loved, one of these boys who is more than capable of burning me if I let them. But how can I say no with his mouth pressed against mine, hot and hungry? What can I do when my body, my brain and my soul all cry out for his touch, his words, his look? I've never had so many parts of my being in agreement before. Always there was something telling me that what I was doing was wrong. Everything about this feels right. It's like I can finally see the light at the end of the tunnel. I've been in darkness for so long that it's easy for me to recognize this burning color, this brightness that I've been denied for far, too long. Ty McCabe has brought it out of me, and I can't say no. He won't let me say no. *I* don't want to say no.

Ty and I brush our lips against one another, rubbing the heat of our tongues together as our hands touch, explore each other's bodies like we've never touched before. And we haven't, not like this. I've *never* been touched like this before. Not by Noah, not by anyone. I reach my fingers under Ty's shirt and he sits up just enough that I can pull it over his head. I've been wanting to do this for a long, long time. I run my fingers up the hard lines of his belly, tracing his abs with my nail, feeling them contract beneath my touch. He groans and arches his back like he can't stand even the barest brush. I love knowing that I can have this much effect on him, and smile.

"You think you're clever?" he asks me as he reaches down and grabs my wrists, pushes them out to the sides and kisses me on the jaw. He works his way down, towards my neck and breathes heat there, drips molten lava across my skin with every exhale.

"Ty," I moan because I've never had the chance to moan someone's name before. Usually, I don't even know it. "Are you jealous of Noah?" I ask on the tail end of a gasp. Ty is nibbling my skin, biting the soft flesh of my throat, squeezing it between his teeth with just enough pressure that I swear it's going to hurt. It doesn't.

"Fuck Noah," he says as releases my hands and grabs the edge of my shirt, tugging it up and over my head and tossing it across the room. Admittedly, I didn't expect to be in this situation, so I'm wearing an ugly, beige bra with thick straps. Ty grins as I cross my arms over my chest to hide it. "If you hate it so much," he says as he bends down and breathes in my hair. "Why don't we take it off?" Ty slides his hands under my torso and miraculously, it only takes him a second to undo the clasps.

"You've had practice," I say with just a hint of jealousy. Ty's grin relaxes into a smile, but he doesn't say a thing. Instead, he grabs the bra with his fingers and slides it down my arms, dropping it off the edge of the bed while his eyes take in my breasts and the sprinkling of freckles along my chest and shoulders.

"God," he says as he bends down and breathes on my nipples, caresses the flesh around them with his warm hand. "You really are fucking beautiful." I grab his hair suddenly, tangle my fingers in it and pull his mouth to mine. Some cultures believe that a person's soul is in their breath and that by kissing, we're exchanging the deepest parts of ourselves. I'd always thought that was a load of shit. Until now. Until Ty. I wrap my hand around Ty's neck, moaning into his mouth while his hand dives lower and starts at the buttons to my jeans.

I don't fight him, letting my fingers explore his back and shoulders, slide across the nape of his neck. It's such a high for me that I groan in disappointment when he moves away, stands up and drops his pants to the floor just like that.

"No fair," I tell him as he slides his hands up my legs and wraps his fingers around the waist of my jeans. "I wanted to take those off."

"Next time," Ty says as he yanks my pants off and tosses them to the floor, leaving me in nothing but a pair of thin, white cotton panties. They're boyshorts, so they're not terribly hideous, but if I had known I was going to be on my back in Ty McCabe's apartment, I would've worn lace. When Ty climbs back on the bed, he sits up for a moment, lets me a get a full, glorious view of his muscular body, the curves of the muscles in his arms and thighs, the smooth skin of his chest and belly and the sweep of dark hair around his cock.

"Guess what?" I tell him as he positions himself between my legs and presses the heavy weight of his body into mine. The bed creaks, shifts, makes this little nest where it's just me and Ty and a bundle of sheets and pillow. "You're fucking beautiful, too." Ty bits my lower lip, sucks it between his teeth and pulls back.

"That's it?" he jokes. "Just beautiful? Not handsome or hung or – " I bite Ty's lip ring, tug on it and twirl it around in my mouth while he groans and reaches down, pushes my panties aside with his ringed fingers. Ty and I are stupid, but we're also infatuated with one another, so we don't bother to use a condom. When he pushes into me, all I can see are stars, and I forget about the things I've learned in our meetings, the fear I felt sitting on those plastic chairs in that clinic, all I can think about is Ty. Ty. Ty.

"Never," he says as my eyes tear up. I don't know why.

I've never cried during sex before. Ty kisses the drops away and moves his body in a gentle rhythm, slides into me with long strokes that cut right to the core, but in a good way, a better way. This isn't a frantic fuck in the back of a frat house. This is me and Ty getting to know one another, touching, feeling, embracing. I look up at the ceiling and wrap my hands around his neck, certain that there won't be another day that I feel like this. It's too good, too perfect. Nothing like this ever lasts; I know that better than anyone. I want to tell him to stop, to get off of me, to go away, but I can't speak.

When the pressure breaks, when I clench Ty's body with mine and listen to him cry out, when I feel his body relax into me, the world gets flipped upside down and won't go back the other way. Something inside of me has changed. If I can accept that, I'll be okay. If not, then I might as well have stayed the way I was, never bothered to try, because if I try to go back, I will break.

"Never," Ty says as he looks down at me and tries to get my attention. I think I'm sobbing but just a bit, just because I'm confused and lost. This is all new territory for me. Fucking and making love are different things, I can see that now. "Are you alright?" he asks me with a small laugh. When he sees that I really am upset, Ty pushes my hair from my face and locks his dark eyes with mine. "Hey, you," Ty says with a wink and a kiss to the cheek. "Promise me you'll never be sad for me or about me." He brushes my tears away and kisses me hard and possessive on the lips. "Promise me that."

"I promise," I say as I take Ty into my arms and into my heart. From where I sit, there's no going back now. My life is now in the hands of fate.

31

I'm sitting on Ty's couch, still naked, with my phone in one hand and a glass of wine in the other. I have *never* felt like this after sex before, so … fulfilled. I've been seeking it out since I left Noah sleeping in my bed at my mother's house, and I haven't found it, not even close. Until now. Until Ty fucking McCabe. I'm staring at the text message, debating whether I should delete it or not. Debating if I should go home or not.

If I do, I might be able to heal some of the rifts in my heart, get to know my sisters, have a family again. I might be able to tell Mom the truth with conviction, and if that bastard is still around, maybe I can finally find justice for my dad? At the same time, there's a lot of room for error there, a lot of chances to fuck things up royally. Besides, if I go home now, I'll have to see Noah. I'll just have to. And I'll have to leave Ty, here, alone. It might only be for a month, but a lot can happen in four weeks. I set my phone aside and take a deep breath. Honestly, it's hard to be stressed when I feel so good, physically, emotionally, even spiritually.

"I'm in love with a guy who wears a nose ring," I say aloud and chuckle. He's dead asleep right now with his tight, little ass peeking out of the blankets, the smooth muscles of his upper back lit up with the silver light from the moon outside the window. Or at least I thought he was.

"Did I hear the word *love*?" Ty asks as he moves into the living room, stark naked. He's beautiful, chiseled and hard, masculine and strong, like a statue of Apollo or some other virile, young god. It's a strange thought to have, but I can suddenly imagine why he worked as a prostitute. I can see why people would be clamoring to pay him for his time. Ty is the most flawed, most tortured, most beautiful human being I have ever met.

This scares me.

I watch him come around the edge of the couch and sit next to me.

"I think you just misheard me," I try to tell him as he yawns and rubs his hand down his belly.

"Did I?" he asks, but he doesn't sound like he believes me. I glance over at the phone and sip my wine.

"What would you do?" I ask Ty as he rubs his eyes and looks at me with sleepy satisfaction. He scoots closer to me and can't seem to keep his hands off my bare skin. I don't know what to think about it because I've never really had a *lover.* I've had sexual partners galore but never a lover, never someone that wanted to hold me, possess me, consume me. Ty wants all of these things and more. "What would you do if the people you loved betrayed you?"

"I've never been in love before," he tells me with a yawn. "So that's a bit outside my range of knowledge, but if you're talking about your family, I think you should go see them." I stare at him, and I wonder if I'm reading too much into his words. *He's never been in love?* What about now? What about the way I'm feeling? Doesn't he feel that way, too? My heart clenches tight, but I try to keep smiling. Ty doesn't notice any of this. He kisses my neck and whispers in my ear. "Come to bed with?" I nod, but my mind is going a hundred miles an hour. When he gets up, he tries to drag me with him and I hold up my wine like it's some kind of stupid fucking explanation.

"Let me finish this, and I'll be right there," I tell him, and he's so cute and naked and tired that he just nods and leans down for a kiss. I wrap my hand around his neck and make it last, burn it into my brain and my heart and my soul. When Ty pulls away, I keep a smile plastered to my face. When he disappears, I frown. I'm having a crisis of character, as Ty would say. Maybe it's because of Noah? No, that's just a convenient excuse. I'm panicking because I'm in deep, because it has just hit me how important Ty has become, and he's the only thing I have now. If something goes wrong, I don't know what I'll do. I know as soon as I start to cry that I'm not thinking clearly, that I'm making a terrible decision. I've been making all the right ones lately and now I'm having a relapse. It happens, with alcoholics, drug addicts, food addicts. It's happening because I don't know how to handle my feelings properly. Of course, like with everything, it has to get worse before it get better.

I finish my wine, get up, get dressed and leave.

32

I'm already at the bus stop when Ty finds me.

I'm standing under the corrugated metal roof that protects the single bench from the rain. In one hand, I have an unlit cigarette that I put between my lips, just so I can hold something there and forget what it was like to have Ty's mouth on mine. I squeeze my eyes shut and feel drops of water run down my eyebrows and slide down the sides of my face.

Tears threaten, but I push them back, determined to keep my promise to Ty. Even if I never see him again, I'll always keep my promise. If I've learned anything in the past few weeks, it's that integrity and honesty are all we really have. Once we lose sight of them, it's just a slow descent into madness. Despite all the odds, I've climbed out of that misery. I'm standing in the light now, and I refuse to go back to the darkness.

I clench my fist around the handle of my suitcase and open my eyes to the sheet of rain that's falling all around me, splashing the dirty pavement and pinging off the roofs of nearby cars. On one side of me is a woman in a leather jacket with haunted eyes and a ghostly smile on her face. On the opposite side is a guy who's determined to tell me his life story, whether I want to hear it or not. I tune out his voice, turn my thoughts to their maximum volume and let them continue to convince me that this is the right thing to do. I've been away from home for far too long. It's time to see my mom and my sisters again, to visit my father's grave, to start over. *It's not too late.* Besides, I'm being overdramatic. I'll be back after break, so it isn't like I won't ever see him again. I swallow hard and try to remember to keep breathing.

"I can never go back," says the man, and I turn my face slowly to look at him. He isn't looking back at me; his gaze is focused out towards the street, but he isn't seeing it. I recognize that expression. He's looking inside of himself, trying to find a reason to be alive. I want to tell him it's okay, that if he tries really, really hard, that he'll find it, but that's his conclusion to come to on his own. I found my reason. I found a whole bunch of reasons and that's why I can't stay here another second. "I can never go back," the man says again, trying to convince himself that it's true. I once thought that, too, but I know that it isn't. You can always go back.

Sometimes, it's just easier to pretend that you can't.

"Never say never," says a voice just outside of my peripheral vision. The tears I've been holding back spill out, run down my face like rain. My lip trembles a bit and the cigarette falls to the ground, lands in a puddle at my feet. Footsteps splash across the pavement towards me and suddenly, there he is with his wet hair in his face and a suitcase in his hand.

"Fuck off," the man tells Ty and stands up, turning away from the two of us and slumping down on the ground on the opposite side of the bench.

"Guess he isn't ready for that kind of advice," Ty says to me, just a blur in my watery vision. I'm trying so hard not to look at him because if I do, I'll never be able to look away again. I'm in love, big time. I've fallen so hard for Ty that if I don't get away now, I'll never be able to get back up. Ty adjusts himself and puts the suitcase down. "But I wasn't talking to him, anyway, I was talking to you."

"Go away," I say, but I don't really mean it, and he can tell.

"Is this seat taken?" Ty asks as he points to the bench, rings and bracelets jangling, dripping water across the last bit of dry pavement that there is. I don't answer him. "Never," he says again and I look up at the sky, eyes so full of tears that I can barely see it. "You can't run away," he tells me as he steps close enough that the toes of our shoes are brushing together.

"I wasn't running away," I tell him. "I'm going home. I have to go home, Ty. There are so many loose ends that I have to tie up. If I leave them hanging, there's a chance I might get tangled up, and I don't want that ever again." He smiles and my heart breaks in two. When he reaches a hand up and tries to cup my face, I turn away.

"Don't," I say, convinced that if he touches me, I'll shred

my ticket and never leave his side again. He doesn't listen; Ty never listens. He slides his fingers across my chin and even though they're cold and wet, they're still warm somehow. It doesn't make any sense, but it's true. "Ty," I breathe as his other hand comes up and tangles in my hair. Then his mouth is on mine, hot and desperate, and I'm dropping my suitcase to the ground and reaching up, pressing my hands into the soggy fabric of his T-shirt.

"Never," he says, pausing for just a moment with his lips pressed into the skin of my forehead. "You're so fucking stubborn sometimes." I shake my head and dodge his next kiss, determined to say what I need to say.

"You said you've never loved anyone, Ty, but I have, and I still do. I have to go home and make things right, and I can't just dismiss my feelings anymore. I love you, and I can't stand around and watch you not loving me." He chuckles and I nearly sock him in the face for it. Instead, he grabs my hand and presses a kiss to my trembling fingertips.

"You misunderstood what I was trying to say. I said I've never loved anyone *before,* meaning before this moment, because Never, I love someone now."

"Who?" I ask and Ty laughs again, pressing his forehead against mine.

"Oh come on," he says, but I won't let it go, not anymore. I need to hear it now, from this person, this way.

"Say it," I tell him as more tears fall and I find myself wondering what the hell I was doing running away from my best friend, from the person who helped me see the light. I might be getting better, but I guess I still have a lot to learn.

"I love you, Never," Ty says, and I bite my lip to keep my emotions in check. They're all swirling around inside of me, flickering like fireflies and lighting up my soul. "Now, promise you'll take me with you," Ty pleads, and I nod because I'm having a hard time speaking through the kisses and the feel of his hands in my wet hair. “Thank god,” he says. “Because I put in a notice at my apartment this morning. If you'd have turned me down, I would've had nothing to go back to.” I laugh, but it's all wrapped up in tears and doesn't sound very pretty. “Now, kiss me again,” he commands and I do.

If you enjoyed this book, look for
Broken Pasts!

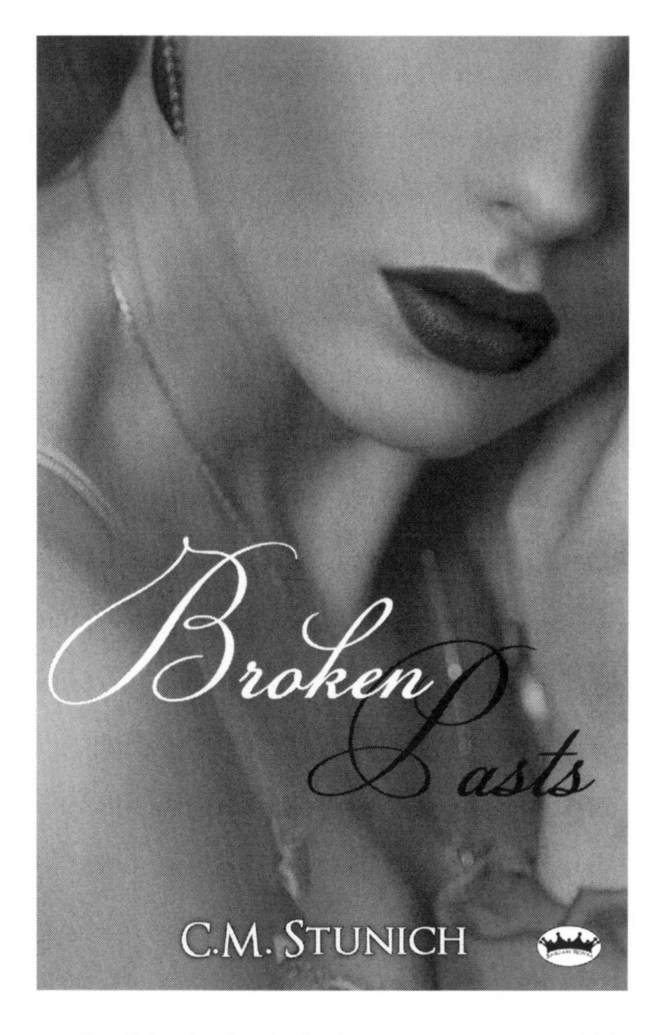

"Until Nathaniel Sutherland was open and all his soul was bared for me to see, I wouldn't be satisfied."

About the Author

C.M. Stunich was raised under a cover of fog in the area known simply as Eureka, CA. A mysterious place, this strange, arboreal land nursed Caitlin's (yes, that's her name!) desire to write strange fiction novels about wicked monsters, magical trains, and Nemean Lions (Google it!). She currently enjoys drag queens, having too many cats, and tribal bellydance.

She can be reached at author@cmstunich.com, and loves to hear from her readers. Ms. Stunich also wrote this biography and has no idea why she decided to refer to herself in the third person.

Happy reading and carpe diem!

www.cmstunich.com